*Blaire had learned dating someone from work never works, but...*

Burke slipped an arm behind her back. His other hand cupped her cheek. His eyes, darkened with emotion, held hers in a powerful gaze. "I think there's something we didn't finish." His voice turned husky. He tightened his grip.

Everything in her ached for his embrace. Blaire tilted her head back. She leaned forward. A picture of Richard flashed through her mind. She closed her eyes. She could see the E-mail he'd sent, telling her the engagement was off. Pain ripped through her heart.

Burke's warm lips covered hers. She jerked her head back. Stiffening her arms, she pushed away from him. Ignoring the hurt in his eyes, she backed off. Burke let go of her.

"I think I need to go back home and change into dry clothes." She knew the excuse was lame. She wanted to fall back into his arms, but she couldn't do that. She refused to go back on her promise to herself. Never again would she fall for someone she worked with.

**NANCY J. FARRIER** resides in Arizona with her husband, son, and four daughters. She is the author of numerous articles and short stories. Her days are busy with home-schooling her daughters. Nancy feels called to share her faith with others through her writing.

**Books by Nancy J. Farrier**

HEARTSONG PRESENTS
HP415—Sonoran Sunrise

Don't miss out on any of our super romances. Write to us at the following address for information on our newest releases and club information.

Heartsong Presents Readers' Service
PO Box 719
Uhrichsville, OH 44683

# An Ostrich
# a Day

*Nancy J. Farrier*

*Heartsong Presents*

To my Lord, who gave the gift of laughter and the Bible, His Word, that guides my steps.

Thank you to my daughters, Anne and Abigail, who love to edit my books.

To Steve and Mitzi Stumbaugh. Thank you for sharing your knowledge of ostriches and for all the fascinating stories.

**A note from the author:**
*I love to hear from my readers! You may correspond with me by writing:* **Nancy J. Farrier**
**Author Relations**
**PO Box 719**
**Uhrichsville, OH 44683**

ISBN 1-58660-380-9

**AN OSTRICH A DAY**

All Scripture quotations, unless otherwise noted, are taken from the King James Version of the Bible.

*Cover illustration by Greg Roman*

PRINTED IN THE U.S.A.

## one

Blaire Mackenzie stepped from her rental car and frowned at the barren Arizona hills surrounding her newly inherited piece of desert. *Barren, just like my life.* She sighed. *Well, not as desolate as the Sahara.*

Prickly cacti, standing stiff and erect like sentinels, marched across the hills, and scrub brush of some sort covered the ground. Blue lupine and California poppies dotted the hillsides. What had the man at the gas station said? The spring flowers were in full bloom, making the desert a garden? Obviously, his idea of a garden didn't agree with the lush flowers found in the Midwest where Blaire hailed from.

An ostrich ranch! Blaire shook her head. Why in the world had her uncle thought she would want to live in this desert and raise ostriches of all things? Who wanted to live around a bunch of overgrown chickens that laid such huge eggs you couldn't even eat them? She'd read an article about these birds. One ostrich egg equaled twenty-four chicken eggs. Who could eat that much for breakfast? How many pound cakes would you have to make to use one egg? The thought boggled the mind.

A strong afternoon breeze whipped Blaire's hair across her face and pulled at her full skirt like a mischievous child. Taking a deep breath, Blaire had to admit there were some advantages to being in the middle of nowhere. The absence of exhaust fumes and the utter quiet gave her the feeling of stepping into another time. At least March in southern Arizona shouldn't bring surprise snow flurries or constant rain.

She wiped a wavy strand of hair off her face, while her other hand tried to smooth her blowing skirt. Was Arizona always this windy? Blaire watched in amazement as a minia-ture brown tornado moved across the nearby pasture, head-ing toward the hills. The sandy cyclone picked up bits of debris, distributing dust and plant fragments in another area as the turbulence wound down.

*God, I don't know how this could be the place You planned for me to live. There must be a mistake here somewhere.* Blaire's gaze wandered across the pens of ostriches. The long-necked birds peered over the fence at her with their comical faces. *How could anyone be happy here, Lord? There isn't even a shopping mall within fifty miles.*

Stepping aside, Blaire swung the car door shut. A young man approached, and Blaire took the opportunity to study him. Would this be the foreman, Burke Dunham? No, she decided. A foreman would be older. The dark-complected youth walking toward her looked like he could still be in high school.

Blaire straightened her shoulders and took a deep breath. "Okay, girl," she muttered softly to herself. "Time to make a good first impression."

"Hello, may I help you?" The young man smiled as he greeted her. His warm brown eyes and white teeth sparkled in the afternoon sunlight. Windblown black hair framed his youthfully handsome face.

"Hello." Blaire attempted a nervous smile as she raked the blowing hair back from her face. Thankfully her skirt wasn't trying to fly off over her head anymore. "I'm looking for Burke Dunham. I'm Blaire Mackenzie, Ike's niece."

"I'm Manuel Ortega. My mother and I worked for your uncle. I'm sorry about your uncle Ike. He was a good man." Manuel grinned and extended his hand. "We've been looking forward to you coming."

Blaire relaxed and stepped forward to shake hands with Manuel. In midstep she realized why her skirt wasn't blow-ing anymore. Caught in the car door, the material tightened around her legs, clamping them in its cottony embrace. Blaire swung forward. Her foot slipped in the sandy dirt. Her arms flailed like an out-of-control windmill. She fought to regain her balance. With a gasp, Blaire realized her face was about to meet the Arizona sand.

A large hand gripped her arm like a vise, and Blaire, pulled upright, found herself looking into a pair of eyes the color of the sea on a moody day. Aqua. Sea-green. Her favorite color. Blaire pushed back from the man and his wonderful eyes only to be caught once more by the confines of her trapped skirt.

"Let me help." The deep rich voice echoed with a tinge of amusement at her predicament. With one hand still on her arm, he reached over and did what she should have done two minutes earlier. He opened the car door, releasing her skirt to play with the wind once more.

Immediately, Blaire stepped back and reached down to keep her skirt from becoming a head scarf. She could hear Manuel chuckling and felt the heat of a blush as she watched her rescuer grin in amusement. A worn, gray cowboy hat shaded his incredible eyes.

He stretched out a hand to her. "Hi, I'm Burke Dunham, the foreman here. I believe I heard you tell Manuel you're Ike Mackenzie's niece."

Blaire nodded. "That's right. I guess I own this ranch now." She lifted her chin, trying to regain a little confidence in front of this much-too-handsome man she would be required to work with. He lifted his hat and brushed his hand over short, straw-colored hair. The cleft in his chin reminded her of her mother's favorite movie star. He settled his hat, and his muscular arm dropped to his side as she stepped away. Standing back a little, she found it easier to look at him without having to tilt her head back so far.

"Well, Miss Mackenzie." Burke spoke seriously. "I know Manuel's a good worker, one of the best, but you don't have to throw yourself at his feet."

Manuel laughed, and Blaire knew her face must be bright red. She wanted to do something totally childish such as slap the smug look from Burke's face or give him a swift kick in the shins. Instead, she heard the voice of her mother saying, "Pride goeth before destruction, Blaire," and she remembered her resolve to make a good impression.

Swallowing her pride, Blaire managed a small smile. "Thank you for helping me out, Mr. Dunham."

A truck pulling a long trailer rumbled down the driveway, road dust boiling out from under the tires. After it ground to a halt, Manuel and Burke both waved at the driver, who stepped down from the cab. "Excuse us for a minute, Miss Mackenzie." Burke nodded at Blaire. "This truck is here to pick up some ostriches. I'll help Manuel get started with the loading, then I'll come and show you around. I'll only be a few minutes."

Blaire watched as Manuel and Burke greeted the driver of the truck like an old friend. They gestured down a side lane, then headed that way as the man climbed back in the vehicle. The truck and trailer clattered down the road, following Manuel and Burke like an overgrown puppy dog, obscuring the two men in the windblown dust.

Blaire sighed, blinked away the image of mesmerizing aqua eyes, and looked across the top of her car at the ranch house. The one-story adobe building sprawled beneath several stately trees. Their branches draped gracefully over the house in an apparent attempt to ward off the sun's heat. A covered porch ran the length of the house, complete with a swing to enjoy on balmy evenings. Trumpet vines covered the latticework at the ends of the porch, their orange blossoms making a bright pattern in the green leaves.

Six months ago, Blaire would have laughed uproariously if anyone had suggested she move to the middle of nowhere and take over her uncle Ike's ostrich ranch. Blaire had intended to continue her career with Bennett and Sons, an accounting firm. Of course, her engagement to Richard Bennett, the son of the firm's founder and its current owner, had meant she would someday be quitting her accounting career to begin another one as a wife and mother. Blaire had looked forward to that time.

Then four months ago that world fell apart. Richard left town with the firm's secretary—and they weren't traveling on business. He sent Blaire an E-mail telling her the engagement was off. An E-mail of all things. He didn't even have the courage to tell her his decision to her face. Without returning home, Richard closed the firm just after Christmas, putting all the employees out of jobs. Blaire had cried until she could barely see out of swollen eyes, feeling as if her life were over before it even began.

*O God, only You know how much he hurt me.* Blaire blinked her eyes to clear the tears as she remembered the sidelong glances of the office workers and the whispered conversations that ended as soon as she entered a room.

For the last three months, Blaire had worked non-stop for a tax preparer, doing taxes for senior citizens who were homebound or in nursing homes. Blaire prayed constantly for the Lord to show her where He wanted her and what He wanted her to do with her life.

When she'd learned of Uncle Ike's death and of the ranch she'd inherited, Blaire was positive that this was her answer to prayer. She'd made arrangements to have her things shipped to Arizona, tied up all the loose ends, and fled the Midwest, where all her hopes and dreams lay scattered. But when she met with the lawyers in Phoenix, Blaire discovered her dreams of cows and grass-carpeted hills didn't match the reality of her inheritance. Uncle Ike had left her a dry, dust-covered ranch full of giant birds.

Turning from the house, Blaire walked toward the nearest pen of ostriches. Three birds stood in the pen. Two were lighter in color. The third ostrich was the largest. His dark-feathered wings waved slightly as he stalked regally around the pen as if trying to impress the world with his importance.

"You must be named Richard," Blaire said to the strutting, dark-feathered ostrich. "You swagger around like you're God's gift to the human race and everyone should be impressed. Well, I'm not awed by you, your majesty."

The female ostriches moved closer to the fence, and Blaire grimaced. "Well, here's Vanessa, the secretary. Yep, same long eyelashes, except these might be real." Blaire leaned forward to get a better look. "My, my, Vanessa, you sure do have knobby knees. Maybe you should wear your feathers a little longer." Shaking her head, Blaire sighed. "I must be going batty. Here I am talking to a bunch of stupid birds."

Blaire strolled on, finding a pen with young ostriches stalking around in miniature imitation of the regal adults. Their feathers looked as soft as down, and Blaire reached through the fence as they came close, trying to see if they felt as soft as they looked. "Ouch!" Blaire jerked her hand away and rubbed her thumb where the young bird had snapped at it. "You guys don't have any teeth," Blaire said, glaring at the young ostriches, "but you sure do have some strong jaws. I guess it's a good thing you're toothless."

The birds crowded close to the fence, tilting their heads from side to side as if trying to understand exactly what Blaire was saying. She smiled and held one hand up in the air. All the little heads followed her hand, reaching toward it with their beaks. With her other hand, Blaire quickly reached through the fence and gently touched one of the ostriches. The stiff, prickly outer quills poked her fingers. Slipping her hand farther through the fence, Blaire could reach the soft, downy under-feathers of the baby ostrich.

"Ah-ha!" Blaire grinned. "I gotcha that time. At least this proves I'm smarter than an ostrich. I guess you guys don't care too much, do you?" The little heads all tilted to one side in unison as if considering whether they cared or not. Blaire laughed and walked back toward the pens of adult ostriches.

&

Manuel grinned at Burke. "The new boss sure is a pretty one."

Burke laughed. "I have to agree she's better looking than Ike. We'll see how she works out. I don't know if someone from the big city will enjoy living here in the middle of the desert."

As Manuel moved toward the pen of ostriches, Burke stood momentarily lost in thought about his new boss. Once again he could see her clear blue eyes. Wide as the Arizona sky on a summer day, those eyes and her heart-shaped face were perfectly framed by thick waves of ash blond hair. Despite her slender frame, Blaire exuded confidence and an air that left no doubt about her ability to handle herself in just about any situation.

"Well, maybe not any situation," Burke chuckled as he remembered a blue-flowered skirt trapped in a car door. *Looks like she may fit in here after all,* he thought.

&

Blaire studied the huge birds with their beautiful long-lashed eyes and slender, graceful necks. She assumed the dark-feathered one was the male. He slowly waved his black-brown wings tipped with white and strutted proudly around the pen, eyeing Blaire as she watched him. The smaller females, with their lighter, grayish-brown coloring, hovered near the nest on the far side of the pen.

Blaire stepped back as the male ostrich stalked past the fence where she stood. He paused, tilting his head to one side, and watched her intently as if warning her not to come too close to his domain.

"Who do you think you are, Buster?" Blaire drew herself up to her full five foot two inches and tried to stare the ostrich down. "I happen to be in charge here now, so you'd better mind your manners." Blaire grinned in triumph as the ostrich moved on, continuing to strut around the pen toward the females.

He slowly fanned his wings as he walked. Blaire watched as one of the long, grayish-white under-feathers drifted to the ground. She moved around the fence and knelt down, hoping to reach the long plume and pull it to her. Unfortunately, the feather remained out of reach, and the wind appeared to have died down for the moment.

Keeping an eye on the ostriches, Blaire moved to the gate and lifted the latch. All three birds were across the pen, apparently ignoring her as they silently discussed something among themselves. Perhaps she could slip inside the pen, retrieve the feather, and be out before they even noticed her.

She slipped the gate open and stepped through, her heart pounding. The silky feather beckoned to her as it lay on the ground only a few feet away. Blaire inched across the pen, then bent to pick up the long downy plume. As she stood, she looked up once more to check on the ostriches before she made her escape from the enclosure.

To her horror, the male ostrich was racing toward her at an incredibly fast pace. His wings were spread and his mouth opened as if sounding a silent battle cry. Blaire stood frozen, unable to take her eyes from the enraged bird bearing down on her. Time slowed. She knew she wouldn't be able to escape this ostrich and his malicious intentions.

A strong arm grasped Blaire around the waist and jerked her off her feet. In a wild dance, someone whirled her around and waltzed her through the gate of the pen before she knew what had happened. Tilting her head back, Blaire looked up into aqua eyes, noticing for the first time how they faded to gray-green at the edges. The eyes flashed with anger, and she flinched despite her resolve to always be strong.

"What do you think you're doing?" Burke exploded as he slammed the gate shut behind them. "Are you trying to get yourself killed?"

## two

Blaire tore herself from Burke's arms. "Of course I wasn't trying to get myself killed," she retorted, waving her hand in a futile attempt to clear away the cloud of dust stirred up by the ostrich's flying feet.

"Then just what were you doing in that pen?" Burke glared at her through narrowed eyes. "Don't you know a male ostrich that size could kill you with one kick?"

Blaire felt faint at the thought of being so close to death. "I. . .I only wanted the feather." A mixture of guilt and anger washed over her, and she stalked across to a pen containing three female ostriches. The curious birds stood near the fence, watching closely as Burke followed her. Blaire feigned interest in the ostriches, hoping Burke would drop the subject and remember his promise to show her around.

Burke took a deep breath and rapped his hat against his leg to knock off the dust. He raked a hand through his short-cropped hair before slamming the hat back on his head. "The ostrich was only defending his territory and his mates. He didn't stop to consider whether you intended to harm them." Softening his tone, he continued. "Until you learn the ropes, ask before you go into a pen, please. Once you get to know your way around, you'll be fine."

Blaire glanced up at him, nervously running the soft feather through her fingers. Her breath caught in her throat as she met his mesmerizing aqua eyes. The intensity of his gaze bored right through her as if he could read her thoughts. She looked down without speaking, chiding herself for acting like a tongue-tied teenager. She wanted to feel anger, yet

13

she knew he was right. She shouldn't have been in the pen.

*God, what is happening here? You know I didn't want to ever be attracted to a man again after Richard. I don't even know Burke, and yet he has me stammering and feeling like a fool.*

Blaire backed a few steps away from Burke, trying to distance herself from him, hoping to regain her composure.

"Miss Mackenzie." Burke stretched out a hand toward her, and Blaire stepped away even farther, her back coming up against the fence of the ostrich pen.

A sudden pain in her scalp caused Blaire to gasp and blink back tears. Again and again the jolt of pain shot through her. She lifted her hands to her head in an effort to figure out what had grabbed her hair and tried to step away, but something held her in place. Burke moved closer and reached his hand toward her. She wanted to dodge but remained helpless to move her head as it snapped tight against the fence. It felt as if her scalp were being pulled in several directions at once.

"Owww!" Blaire yelled.

Once more Burke came to her rescue, the corners of his mouth struggling not to tip upward in a smile. Reaching above her head, Burke grabbed an ostrich and forced it to release Blaire's hair from its beak. A hunk of ostrich-gummed hair fell in Blaire's face, but once more her head was jerked back.

"Shoo now! Get out of here," Burke yelled at the ostriches, waving his hands to distract them. The others loosed their hold on Blaire and moved back into the pen.

"Are you okay?" Burke's mouth quivered. His jaw clenched as if he were trying not to laugh at her.

Blaire imagined the spectacle she must make. Her hair would be sticking out in all directions, ostrich slobber, if they did such a thing, shining on the dark blond waves. Her face must be as red as a candy apple. *O God, I certainly made an impression here. I'm so glad I won't be staying long.*

As Blaire looked at Burke, who fought to keep from laughing, she glanced over at the ostriches and swore she could see a smirk on their silly bird faces. It was too much. First she grinned, then chuckled, and before she knew it she was grasping her sides, doubled over with laughter. Burke joined her as he led her a safe distance from the pen.

"Are you okay?" Burke gasped again when they'd calmed down enough to talk. "They pulled your hair pretty hard." At that they both dissolved into giggles again.

Finally, Blaire could control her laughter enough to be able to admit, "I'm fine. My head is a little sore, but at least I still have some hair left." She rubbed her scalp and ran her fingers through her hair in an attempt to get it back in a semblance of order. "Thank you, once again, for rescuing me. I'm not sure how I'll manage here. I don't know what Uncle Ike was thinking, leaving this place to me."

"I think Ike knew exactly what he was doing." Burke's low, rich voice still held a hint of amusement. "Ike used to talk about you a lot. He always wanted you to come to visit. He said you stole his heart when you were a baby and would crawl on his lap and fall asleep. He talked about your blond curls and blue eyes and said you could get him to do anything for you. Is that right?"

Blaire smiled, remembering how Uncle Ike always treated her like a queen. "Before Uncle Ike traveled, we were very close." Blaire frowned. "Then he started moving around the country, going from one job to another. We didn't see much of him because he barely gave us his new address before he moved to another place. A couple of times he showed up at our house for a short visit. I always missed him."

"He was a good man," Burke agreed. "Come on, I'll show you around the ranch. Ike bought this place five years ago and worked hard to build it up. He's done a remarkable job considering the opposition he faced and the state of neglect the place was in when he bought it."

"Opposition?" Blaire questioned.

Burke shrugged. "Oh, you know, raising ostriches in cattle country just isn't done. But your uncle did everything with such grace that he won a lot of friends in a short time. Come on, let's start over here with the hatchery."

Burke led the way to an oblong shed and unlocked the door. Blaire followed him into a small room equipped with several pairs of clean sandals and a sink for washing. "Ostrich eggs are easily contaminated, so if you ever handle them, you must wash your hands first. If your shoes are dirty, slip them off and put on a pair of these sandals."

Blaire nodded, then peered through the glass of the door leading into the next room. Several large metal incubators lined the walls. She could see the huge, cream-colored ostrich eggs resting side by side, waiting to hatch out.

"What are all the lights on the wall by the door?" Blaire indicated a panel of lights with digital numbers glowing beside them.

"Those show the temperature of each incubator. We check these several times a day. We have to maintain the temperature at 97.5, and if it dips too low or goes too high an alarm sounds outside and in the house."

"How many eggs do you get every day?"

Burke frowned in thought. "Well, we have forty-two breeders—females that are laying fertilized eggs—and they each lay an egg every forty-eight hours. We get approximately twenty-one eggs a day and put most of them in the incubators. The infertile eggs are blown out and sold to a lady in Tucson."

"What does she do with the eggs?"

"She decorates them, does etchings, then sells them. She makes some beautiful lamps out of the eggs."

"So about how many eggs are fertile?"

Tilting his head back, Burke frowned for a moment. "I think we get an average of eighteen fertile eggs a day."

Blaire's eyes widened. "That's a lot of eggs—almost five hundred and fifty a month. There weren't that many ostriches out there. What do you do with them all?"

"You haven't even seen any of the ranch yet. Come on, I'll take you on a little tour."

Burke led Blaire to a fairly new dark-blue pickup and opened the door for her. He flipped the door shut and walked around the truck. Blaire started to pull her skirt out of the way so she could fasten her seat belt. As Burke climbed in on the driver's side, she sheepishly opened her door and pulled the skirt inside the truck. She made a face at Burke. "I guess my skirt just likes doors."

Burke chuckled with her as he drove down a lane between ostrich pens. "We only keep the breeders close to the house. That makes it easier to gather the eggs. Your uncle's property, now yours, extends out through these hills."

They rounded the base of a hill. Blaire gasped. Fenced pastures stretched before her, filled with ostriches of various sizes. "How many are there?" she asked in an awed tone.

"We currently have over twenty-eight hundred birds, not counting the breeders up by the house."

Blaire looked at him in shock. "What did Uncle Ike do with so many ostriches?"

Burke grinned, and she quickly looked back out the window at the fields dotted with ostriches. "Over there," Burke said, pointing out the window, "is our processing plant. There's a growing market for ostrich meat, so a lot of our birds are raised for slaughter. We do sell some of them, too, especially the ones that look like they will be good breeders."

Burke pulled the truck to a stop and climbed out. "Come on," he said as he opened Blaire's door. "You can walk in with these ostriches. The only ones that are really dangerous are the breeders. These are juvenile females."

"They all look big to me," Blaire murmured as they walked toward the pasture gate.

"Just remember to stay out of the pens with males in them, and you'll be fine. Watch out!" Burke grabbed her arm and pulled her toward him. A tingle raced up Blaire's arm, and she tried to pull out of his firm grasp.

"Watch out for what?"

"The cactus." Burke pointed to the prickly plant she had nearly walked into. "This is the desert, and many of the plants here are very unfriendly. It's the only way they can survive. That one, the cholla, is particularly nasty."

Blaire leaned over for a closer look and shuddered at the miniature branches covered with vicious-looking curved barbs. It wouldn't be pleasant to get stuck with those. She glanced back up at Burke. "It seems all I'm doing today is thanking you for saving me from one thing or another." Burke smiled warmly, but before he could say anything she hurriedly added, "I'll be glad when I can get back to the city where life is safer."

Burke's warm smile faded. He turned to open the pasture gate, waited for Blaire to step through, then followed, clicking the gate closed behind them.

The pasture stretched before her, barren of growth, picked clean by hundreds of curious beaks. They were standing in a long valley between low hills. Blue-tinged mountains lifted high in the distance, meeting a skyline that appeared to extend forever. A few white, puffy clouds scudded across the azure sky.

Blaire looked around slowly. There were no tall buildings here, no freeways or bus routes. She couldn't even hear a car engine. The utter quiet could be peaceful, she supposed, if one adjusted to the silence. Blaire didn't think she would ever adapt, and she didn't want to anyway. This wasn't for her. She wanted the excitement of city life, shopping, and the ease of getting anywhere she wanted in a matter of minutes on the convenient freeways.

Blaire closed her eyes for a moment and pictured her favorite mall. Throngs of people crowded through, chattering to one another as they made their purchases or just window-shopped. The hum of voices. The smell of cookies, caramel corn, and candies. The mouth-watering aroma of various ethnic foods. Blaire could almost smell her favorite Mexican dishes.

The smile blossoming on Blaire's face faded as she recalled her last trip to the mall. She and Richard had walked arm in arm as she chattered nonstop about their wedding. Richard had been unusually quiet that day. Later Blaire realized his thoughts weren't on her and their upcoming wedding; he was thinking only of his plans to dump her and run off with Vanessa.

"Miss Mackenzie?" Blaire jumped as Burke touched her arm. She blinked back tears and fought to clear her memories.

"I'm sorry." She blushed, thinking how stupid she must appear. "I was just comparing the quiet openness of the desert to the city life I'm used to. I don't know how you survive without. . .I mean, where do you shop around here anyway?"

A low, hearty sound rumbled in Burke's chest. "We have peddlers who come by every couple of months and show us their wares. If we get too desperate, we can send out a distress signal and have food air dropped so we don't starve."

Blaire rolled her eyes. "Okay, I deserved that, but you have to remember I'm used to having a grocery store or mall within fifteen minutes of where I live."

"Well, we are a little farther from shopping, but it isn't hopeless. There are stores in Winkelman and Kearny where you can pick up a few things. For major shopping, most people go to Globe, Tucson, or Phoenix. They even have movie theaters and malls, just like they do back East."

Blaire's melodic laugh floated across the quiet pasture. "I guess you adjust to this life, but I'm not sure I ever could."

"Come on." Burke led the way across the pasture. "I want to show you something." They walked toward the largest group of ostriches, dust from the barren ground swirling up around their ankles. "These are all young females around ten months old."

Blaire wrinkled her nose as the dust from shuffling ostrich feet drifted up around them. She fought a losing battle to stop the sneeze that was building. As she lifted her hand to her nose, Burke pulled a brightly colored handkerchief from his hip pocket and handed it to her with a flourish.

In unison the ostriches lifted their long necks to stare at them. They tilted their heads to one side and circled uneasily, then began to edge away. Blaire's sudden sneeze echoed across the pasture.

As one, the young birds stretched out their long legs and ran. More and more of the ostriches joined the first group racing around the barren field, dust flying around them in a cloud. Blaire jumped as Burke leaned close and said, "Just stand still, and we'll be fine. They can reach speeds of up to forty-five miles per hour and can continue at that pace for about twenty minutes."

"Do they do this very often?" Blaire stared in amazement at the racing birds, their strong legs pushing hard and giving them the appearance of floating above the ground. Their wings fanned uselessly beside their bodies.

"Once in awhile something spooks them, and they take off for a run. Then again, sometimes they don't get spooked. Perhaps running feels good."

Once more the young birds raced around the far end of the pasture heading back toward the gate. As they ran opposite Blaire and Burke, the lead bird pivoted and headed straight for them. The other birds followed their leader, and to Blaire's horror, the whole flock of ostriches rushed at breakneck speed toward her. This time the gate was too far away to dash through to safety.

*God, help us,* Blaire silently pleaded as she flung herself at Burke, hiding her face against his chest and trembling in anticipation of being trampled by hundreds of gargantuan chickens.

# three

Burke's arms closed around Blaire, pulling her close against his chest. A lemony scent wafted up from her, and for a moment he felt the temptation to bury his nose in her hair. His jaw clenched in an effort to avoid being affected by this attractive woman.

A swirl of dust drifted over the pair as the young ostriches skidded to a halt. Nosy beaks tugged at their clothing. Burke made himself release Blaire as she pushed away from him. Her widened eyes and open mouth told him more than words of her surprise to still be standing and not squashed under ostrich feet.

"They stopped," Blaire gasped.

Burke chuckled. "I wouldn't bring you anywhere you'd be in danger. These young ladies won't hurt you, although if you're not careful they can get a little rambunctious with your clothing."

Blaire firmly pushed away an ostrich who was trying to remove her skirt. "Stop that."

"This is worse than the wind, huh?"

Blaire nodded, her sky blue eyes twinkling. "Perhaps she thinks she'll look better in this skirt than I do. I have to admit I'm a little selfish, though. I don't plan to exchange my skirt for her feathers no matter how beautiful they are."

"Before she gets too disappointed, maybe we should continue our tour." Burke led Blaire through the crowd of ostriches. Like a group of nosy schoolgirls, the ostriches followed them to the gate, looking disappointed at being left behind.

Back in the truck, Burke and Blaire rattled over the rutted dirt road as he pointed out the fields filled with various age groups and sexes of ostriches. He showed her the hayfields where they raised much of their own feed and the processing plant where the ostriches were butchered.

"What do you do with all the meat?" Blaire asked as they walked out of the cool building that housed the processing plant.

"We have several markets for the meat across the country. We also sell the skins. Ostrich hides make good leather. In fact, there's a better market for the leather now than the meat. That could change with the problems in the European meat market." He shrugged. "Who knows what will happen there. Now, I'd better show you to the house and get you settled in before Isabel tans my hide."

"Who's Isabel?" Blaire asked as Burke closed her door, walked around the front of the truck, and climbed in on the driver's side.

"Isabel is Manuel's mother," Burke answered as he started the truck and slowly headed back toward the house. "She worked for Ike when he first came here, and Manuel was an ornery high school student. Her husband died in an accident at the mines. I guess Ike was an answer to prayer for her."

"Why is that?"

"Well, she didn't have much family here, and she'd never worked outside the home. Ike not only gave her a job and a home, but he took Manuel under his wing and helped him get straightened out. I sometimes wonder how Manuel would have turned out if Ike hadn't come along. He sure ran with a rough crowd back then."

Blaire leaned her head back against the truck seat, obviously tired. Burke glanced sideways at her, wondering at his attraction to this woman he had just met yet felt he'd known for years. Of course, Ike always bragged about Blaire and showed every picture of her like she was his favorite daughter instead of a niece.

*Lord,* Burke prayed silently, *You know she says she's not staying. Help me not to get attached to her. I don't want to be involved with a woman. They're just trouble, and I don't need that.*

Burke thought of his years growing up. He remembered his mother mostly from her pictures. She'd died when he was eight years old. Sometimes a certain fragrance or phrase she used to say would remind him of how she loved to hold him on her lap and read to him. Mostly, he recalled her leaving him. He could still remember the old feelings of rejection as he stood beside her casket and looked at her still, white face.

His grandmother tried hard to fill in. Burke loved her and slowly trusted her with his deepest hurts and fears. However, just before he turned twelve, he came home from school to find his grandmother lying cold and quiet in the middle of the living room.

Then there was Julie. His jaw clenched until his teeth hurt. He refused to think about Julie.

Since that time Burke hadn't trusted another woman. They all left right when you learned to love them. He didn't want to get involved with a woman and risk the vulnerability that came with it. After experiencing the feelings Blaire evoked, Burke sincerely hoped she would go back to the city as fast as she had arrived.

ঞ

"Come on in." Burke set the suitcase down and opened the door for Blaire. She stepped up beside him, carrying her smaller case and her purse. Gazing in awe at the double doors, Blaire admired the colors in the stained-glass panels at the side of each door. Beautiful lavender irises glittered in the midst of the design of green grasses and blue sky. Tiny yellow-and-orange butterflies hovered over the flowers.

"Your uncle Ike said irises were always his favorite flower." Burke pointed to the glass panels. "He figured this was the best way to have irises all year round."

"They're beautiful," Blaire said. "You can almost see the butterflies' wings moving and hear bees buzzing. Whoever made these stained-glass windows did an excellent job."

Blaire turned to go through the doorway, still thinking of Uncle Ike and his love for flowers, not seeing the step up into the entryway. The toe of her sandal caught on the edge of the step, and she stumbled forward, unable to catch herself because her hands were full. The blur of tile flooring rushed up to meet her before she could even think about what to do.

"Whoa, there." Blaire felt Burke grab her arm, stopping her just as her knees met the floor. "There you go throwing yourself on the ground again." Burke's voice held a hint of amusement.

As Burke helped her to her feet, Blaire could feel the heat of a blush spreading up her face. She turned to look at him. "I guess I have a confession to make." She bit her lower lip, trying to hold back the hysterics. "I'm a complete, total, hopeless klutz." Unable to hold back any longer, she burst out laughing.

Burke joined in her laughter as he reached back outside for her suitcases. "We'd better get you into the living room. At least it has a padded carpet if you feel an urge to throw yourself down again."

Still giggling, Blaire turned to look through the entryway into the long living room. Mexican tile covered the foyer in a half moon shape that led to the rich, brown, variegated living room carpet. Blaire's shoes clicked a loud tattoo as she crossed the tile and turned silent as they sank into the thick carpeting.

The living room was definitely a man's room, complete with polished wood and brown cushioned furniture. A smattering of wildlife prints decorated cream-colored walls. Old-fashioned lanterns and branding irons trimmed the mantel above the fireplace. Heavy wooden beams graced the vaulted ceiling. The room created a down-home feel, and Blaire wanted nothing more than to sink into one of the couches, kick off her shoes, and prop up her feet.

"What is that heavenly smell?" Blaire breathed deeply. Her stomach rumbled, and she realized how hungry she was. After learning the exact nature of her inheritance that morning, she'd been so upset that she'd only managed to eat a little soup and salad for lunch. Now her appetite had returned, and the enticing aromas drifting from the kitchen drew her like a magnet.

Burke took in a long breath, a slight smile lighting his handsome features. "I believe you've gotten a whiff of Isabel's famous enchiladas."

Blaire forced herself to look away as his sparkling eyes met hers. *He works here,* she thought. *I can't be attracted again to someone I work with.* She did her best to ignore the prickle of electricity racing through her.

"Isabel," Burke called. "Miss Mackenzie is here."

A small, stocky woman hurried into the living room, brushing a strand of gray-streaked dark hair from her face. A sheen of sweat lit up her face along with a smile that made Blaire feel more than welcome.

"Miss Mackenzie." Isabel bubbled with excitement. "I've been looking forward to meeting you. I loved your uncle Ike so much." A tear threatened to fall from her warm brown eyes, and she swiped it away with the back of her hand. "I hope you are hungry. The lawyer called and said you were on your way, so I made a special Mexican supper for you."

Burke grinned and leaned over to give the excited woman a quick kiss on her cheek. "Slow down, Isabel, and let me introduce you."

Isabel frowned at Burke and said loftily, "We do not need such formality here. I know who Miss Mackenzie is. She is part of my family. Right, *Mija?*" Isabel's friendly smile warmed Blaire in a way she couldn't describe. She knew she would enjoy getting to know this friend of her uncle.

"Well, I'm not sure what a me-ha is, but I agree we don't need formality. I'm so glad to meet you, Isabel, and yes, I'm starving." Impulsively, Blaire bent down and gave the diminutive woman a quick hug.

"*Mija* is a Spanish term of endearment meaning 'my daughter,' " Burke informed Blaire. "Now if you ladies will excuse me, I'll put these suitcases in Blaire's room and help Manuel with the chores. We should be done in about an hour. Is that okay?" He looked at Isabel.

"That will be fine, *Mijo*." Isabel smiled and patted him affectionately on the cheek. "Why don't you show Miss Mackenzie her room, and she can come to the kitchen when she's ready."

Burke led the way to a door to the right of the living room. He set the luggage down inside the doorway and stepped aside for Blaire to enter. "This was Ike's room, so it isn't very feminine. We didn't redecorate because we didn't know what you would like. I hope the decor is okay for now."

"I love it. Besides, I won't be staying long," Blaire said, turning away from the sudden anger apparent in Burke's green eyes. She turned to gaze in awe at the huge room, mentally comparing it to her small apartment in Illinois. Thick, forest green carpet covered the floor and set off cream-colored walls. The king-size bed in the middle of the room looked more like a twin. A stone fireplace in the outer wall was lined with reminders of her uncle, including a row of pictures on the mantle.

"There's a bathroom through this door." Burke gestured to the left. "The door on the other side of the bathroom leads to the office. Ike recently had a computer installed to keep track of all the ostriches and accounts. I'm afraid he didn't get things caught up. He wasn't the best at doing the book work."

Peeking through the door into the bathroom, Blaire turned back and smiled at Burke. "Maybe I can be useful here for awhile, anyway. As an accountant, doing the books will be my specialty. At least, if I don't fall on top of the computer."

Blaire could hear Burke chuckling until the hall door closed behind him. She sighed as she looked at the huge room that was now hers. *O Lord, I would love to live in a room like this. I love this house, and the people here are so friendly. Why does it have to be in the middle of a desert? I know You don't mean for me to live in a place this desolate.*

Stretched out across the huge, soft waterbed, Blaire sighed in delight as the mattress cradled her tired body. For the first time in weeks she relaxed, nestling on top of the brown striped comforter. Her body grew heavy, and she drifted off to sleep. Twenty minutes later she groaned as she forced herself up off the bed, knowing if she stayed there any longer she would be asleep for the night.

Crossing to the mammoth fireplace, Blaire began to study the pictures on the mantle. Most of them were snapshots of her by herself that her mother had sent to Uncle Ike over the years. The photos were arranged chronologically. In the middle were shots of Blaire and Uncle Ike together before he left on the road, Blaire and her younger brother and sister, and a picture of her family taken for the church directory just before Blaire graduated from high school.

Shrugging off a feeling of melancholy, Blaire unpacked and hung her dresses in the closet. She wanted to visit Isabel in the kitchen. Perhaps talking with Isabel would help her forget the confusing feelings she struggled with. Blaire knew God didn't want her to stay in a place like this, somewhere so foreign to everything she'd grown accustomed to. What she didn't understand were the feelings of contentment that crept in, the desire to settle into this beautiful old house and stay forever.

Following the enticing aromas drifting through the house, Blaire had no trouble finding Isabel. The kitchen, easily as large as Blaire's bedroom, included a dining alcove with a beautiful oak table and matching chairs. Isabel bustled from the rich walnut cabinets to the triple stainless-steel sink. A large pot of something bubbled on the stove, and Blaire could see a couple of cheese-topped dishes baking in the oven.

"Hello," she said hesitantly.

Isabel turned quickly, perspiration shining on her brown face. "Oh, *Mija,* come in and sit down. Can I get you something cool to drink?"

"No thanks, Isabel, I'm fine. Is there something I can do to help with supper?"

"I think the food is about ready. Burke and Manuel should be about done with the chores. I hope you like Mexican food."

Blaire crossed to the stove, peered into the large pot, and breathed in the fragrance. "I love Mexican food, but something tells me I've never had the real thing in Chicago."

Isabel laughed. "Mexican food varies from state to state. We'll have to wait and see if you appreciate Mexican food from this area. I tried not to add too much chili, knowing you were from back East. Did you enjoy your tour of the ranch?"

Blaire leaned against the counter and groaned. "I loved seeing everything, but I'm afraid I made a complete fool of myself today." She sighed and recounted for Isabel all the embarrassing incidents—catching her skirt in the car door, getting her hair pulled, being terrified of the racing ostriches, and finally falling through the doorway to the house.

Isabel laughed and handed Blaire a bowl of jalapeño peppers to set on the table. "I'm sure no one thought you a fool," Isabel assured her.

"I'm positive Burke thinks I'm nothing but a clumsy oaf."

"I don't think that at all." Burke's low voice near her ear startled Blaire.

"Ahh!" she yelled, throwing her hands in the air. Jalapeño peppers flew from the dish like tiny green missiles, scattering across the kitchen floor.

# four

For the next few days, Blaire worked hard at learning her way around the ranch. She wanted to discover the full scope of her inheritance so that she could put the property on the market soon. She quickly realized the number of ostriches and the extensive operations made the operation a sizable legacy from Uncle Ike. Before listing the property with a Realtor, she wanted to know its value—even if that meant staying longer than a few weeks.

Blaire tilted her head and listened to the rumble of a large truck lumbering down the driveway, the vibrations drumming through the floor of the house. Almost daily a variety of vehicles arrived to haul off meat or pick up ostriches sold to other ranches or individuals. The noisy trucks were the one intrusion into an otherwise quiet existence. *Thank You, God, for that bit of noise. Otherwise, the quiet would drive me crazy.*

A knock sounded on her bedroom door. Blaire sighed and set her Bible on the small table next to her. "Coming," she called, as she padded across the soft, thick carpet.

"Good morning, *Mija.*" Isabel's smile lit the room as Blaire opened the door. "There is someone here to see you."

"Me?" Blaire stepped out of the bedroom, wondering who her visitor could be.

"Some men with a big truck say they have brought your belongings." Isabel grinned. "I am so glad that you will be able to make the house more like your own now."

Blaire walked out onto the verandah. Two men were disgorging the contents of the truck she'd heard coming down the driveway. Cardboard boxes of various sizes and a few pieces of furniture were piling up on the porch, neatly balanced one on the other. Movement caught her eye. Over by the ostrich pens Burke and Manuel were walking toward the house, probably wondering what was happening.

"Wait," Blaire called to the movers. "Why did you bring this here?"

The stocky young man closest to her shifted uncomfortably and shoved a hand in the pocket of his coveralls. "We're just following orders, Ma'am. We were told to deliver these goods to this address."

"But I told the lawyers I wanted to keep my things in storage in Phoenix until I decided what to do about the ranch. Can't you take them back?"

"If we take it back and store it, you'll be charged extra." The man scratched his head and gave his partner a bewildered look.

*"Mija,"* Isabel said, "why don't you go ahead and keep your things here? It would be a waste of money to send them back to Phoenix."

Just then, Burke and Manuel arrived. The intensity of Burke's gaze weighed Blaire down. She glanced at him, and like an animal trapped in a glare of light, she couldn't look away. Burke's mouth tipped up, softening his clean-cut features. Released from his magnetic pull, Blaire nodded. "I guess we'll put everything in the spare bedroom until I know where I'll be staying."

Blaire tried to ignore the way Burke's half-smile turned to a scowl. For the past few days he'd seemed to avoid her. Now he looked almost angry as he and Manuel joined in helping unload the boxes.

Before long, the delivery truck was lumbering back down the driveway and out of sight, leaving her precious belongings in a pile for the entire world to see.

"Well, we could form a bucket brigade to get all this stuff

in the house." Burke grinned at Blaire as if trying to present a peace offering.

Blaire forced a smile and nodded. "Either that or we could put up a yard-sale sign."

"I'm sure you have some beautiful things in here, *Mija*." Isabel peered at all the carefully marked boxes. "I think we should just start carrying these in and line them along the bedroom wall."

Manuel picked up a couple of boxes as Burke reached for a small one on top of a stack. "Here's one you can carry, Blaire. It's marked 'personal clothing,' and is it ever heavy," Burke grunted as he slowly lifted the box, his back slightly bent from the effort. "Here, you take it," he called as he heaved the box toward Blaire.

"Wait," Blaire squealed as she reached for the box flying through the air toward her. She braced herself and took a step back as the box thumped against her. Instinctively, she closed her arms tightly around the cardboard carton. Her mouth dropped open in surprise. The box wasn't heavy at all.

Suddenly, she felt something brushing against her legs. She looked down, and her cheeks burned. The bottom of the box had popped open from the force of her hold, and a kaleidoscope of colored underwear and bras had tumbled to her feet. A lacy bra dangled from the bottom of the box, the pink satin bow in the middle of it twinkling in the sunlight. *Oh, please, let this porch open up and swallow me.*

Blaire glanced up to see Manuel biting his lip to keep back the laughter. Burke stared wide-eyed, his mouth hanging open and his cheeks flushed. Horrified, she watched as he lifted his gaze to hers. His mouth snapped shut and his eyes sparkled. Leaning against the boxes, Burke threw back his head and began to laugh.

The heat of embarrassment surged through Blaire as she watched him. She started to turn but stumbled and grabbed a post to catch herself. The mashed box flew through the air and thumped against the house. Colored underwear and lacy bras scattered across the porch. Burke leaned over, grasped his sides, and howled at the sight of the dainty clothing dangling from the swing.

"Here, *Mija,* let me help with that box." Isabel reached for the crumpled box. Her lips twitched, and her eyes flashed with humor. Blaire glanced again at the embarrassing bits of clothing perched haphazardly around her. Unwanted laughter welled up inside. One chuckle slipped out followed by another, and soon they were all in hysterics as Blaire and Isabel rescued the wayward underwear from various perches around the veranda.

After repairing and refilling the box, Blaire carefully carried it into the house and added it to the growing stack. "Well, at least I didn't air my dirty laundry." She grinned. "Those were all clean."

Isabel chuckled. "I know you didn't plan for your things to be shipped here, but why don't we unpack a few boxes? Maybe it will help you feel more at home."

"No." Blaire frowned. "I don't plan to stay longer than needed. I don't want to have to pack again."

Burke straightened from depositing the last of the boxes, his smile vanishing. "What do you plan to do with the ranch?"

"I plan to sell it." Blaire tried to ignore the hurt and anger in Burke's eyes. "I can use the proceeds to open my own accounting firm in Chicago or maybe Phoenix. I've always wanted that."

Burke's eyes were devoid of humor, and his mouth set in a stern line. "What about Isabel and Manuel? If you sell the ranch they won't have a home anymore. Don't you care that they will have nowhere to go when you leave?" He took a deep breath, lifted his hat, and raked his hand through his hair.

"Of course I care. I didn't think about that." Blaire tried

to look away to avoid the discomfort of Burke's gaze. "Uncle Ike was wrong about me. I'm not cut out for country life."

"I guess Ike didn't know you as well as he thought he did." Burke's eyes reflected the sadness of his tone. "Come on, Manuel. We need to finish our other chores." With that he stalked out of the room, followed by Manuel.

Silence settled around her as Blaire stared after Burke's retreating back. She turned to look into Isabel's teary eyes. "I'm sorry, Isabel. I didn't realize your situation. I'm just try- ing to find out what God wants for me to do."

Isabel squeezed Blaire's arm. "It's okay, *Mija*. You have many decisions to make."

Blaire gave Isabel a quick hug, and the older woman smiled, reaching for the repaired box. "You should at least put these underwear in a drawer where they can't get away again."

Blaire looked at the boxes lining the bedroom wall. All her worldly possessions were packed in them. Studying the labels, she walked along the row and picked out three boxes from the stack.

"Help me carry these over next to the bed, and we'll unpack them," she said, handing one of the smaller boxes to Isabel. She picked up the other two and crossed the bedroom.

"This is my collection of giraffes," Blaire explained. "I've been collecting them since my twelfth birthday when Dad and Mom got me this stuffed one." Blaire pulled a well-loved fuzzy giraffe from the box and laid it on her pillow.

"Oh, this one is beautiful." Isabel pulled a carved mother and baby giraffe from the box. The dark wood gleamed. The mother giraffe's long, graceful neck circled over her young one as she bent toward it.

"My sister sent me that one last Christmas. She and her husband are missionaries in Africa. One of the men in her congregation carved it."

"I didn't know your sister is a missionary." Isabel beamed

her approval. "Ike once told me your brother is a pastor."

Blaire nodded, relaxing. For the first time in months, she felt a longing to talk to someone. "My family always went to church. Everyone assumed I would marry a pastor or missionary like my sister." She sat down on the bed, fingering a small glass giraffe. "You know, I knew all the Christian lingo from the time I could talk. I went to church, helped with the nursery when I got older, sang in the choir, and did everything a good Christian should do."

"But you weren't really a Christian, were you?" Isabel sat close to her on the bed.

Blaire glanced up, tears in her eyes. "I wasn't. Everyone thought I was, and they all had such high expectations for me. I let them down." Blaire wiped the tears from her eyes with the side of her hand. "I wanted to be an accountant. I dreamed of having my own business. Then when I went to work at Bennett and Sons and met Richard, I thought my dreams were coming true."

"What happened, *Mija?*"

"We planned to marry. I floated through life those days not seeing the other side of Richard. He charmed me. Blinded to his faults, I didn't realize what was happening until too late. He ran off with the secretary, then closed the firm, putting us all out of work." Blaire continued to talk, telling Isabel of the whispers behind her back and the shame she had suffered.

"The only good thing that came of it was a realization of my need for Jesus. I can remember all the hurt. It was a physical pain." Blaire drew in a shaky breath. "One night I lay on the floor and pictured myself at the foot of the cross. I gave all of myself to Jesus, even though my life wasn't much. I'm trying hard to live as He wants me to live."

Isabel hugged Blaire to her. "Oh, *Mija,* you are all Jesus wants. There is no greater gift you can give Him than your love and your life."

❧

Burke pressed his fingers against the corners of his eyes, trying to stop the moisture threatening to overflow. He eased out of the padded chair in front of the computer in the office, praying it wouldn't squeak and reveal his presence. A high-pitched squeal echoed in the office. He hoped Blaire and Isabel were too distracted to notice. He hadn't meant to eavesdrop on them. He'd only wanted to run in and try to straighten out some of the accounts. Now, all he wanted was some fresh air and the space to distance himself from the hurt in Blaire's voice. No wonder she wanted to get away, to lose herself in the city.

Crossing to the hatchery, Burke wondered at the emotional pain Blaire had endured. How could that cad justify treating her so callously? Anger burned within until he recalled the good that came from the shame. *Lord, I guess sometimes we have to fall flat before You can get our attention. Thank You for reaching out to Blaire. Please heal her wounds. Help her to see that You brought her here for a reason. I don't believe Ike made a mistake.*

Burke washed his hands with disinfectant, donned a pair of clean sandals, and slipped through the heavy door of the incubator room. Checking temperatures, he moved around the room, looking over the oval, ivory-colored eggs. He smiled as he looked in the last incubator. Several of the eggs were cracked, shaking from time to time as the occupants demanded their release. Burke hurried from the room, slipping on his shoes again and heading for the house.

"Blaire." Burke strode through the kitchen door. "Isabel, come here."

The two women stepped out of Blaire's bedroom, their eyes slightly reddened. "What is it, *Mijo?*" Isabel asked.

"It's time." Burke's grin widened at Blaire's look of confusion.

"Time for what?" Blaire asked.

Burke winked conspiratorially at Isabel. "Come with me and find out." He gestured toward the back door.

Isabel nodded in understanding. "You two go ahead. I'll be along shortly."

Blaire followed Burke out the door. Entering the hatchery, Burke pulled off his shoes, slipped on sandals, and told Blaire to do likewise as he began to wash his hands.

"What is going on?" The mystified tone in Blaire's voice made Burke want to laugh.

"I have something to show you." He chuckled as he opened the door to the incubator room. "This is the most exciting time of the year."

Burke stopped in front of an incubator. He reached back, pulling Blaire closer. She leaned forward, gazing at the eggs. Suddenly, she gasped and turned to look at him, her blue eyes wide with delight. "The babies are hatching."

"Yep," Burke agreed. "This is the first hatching of the year. It's always my favorite. Help me move the eggs to the hatching area."

For the next few hours, Blaire watched mesmerized as the baby ostriches pecked their way bit by bit through the tough shells housing them. She gasped in awe when the first little bird tumbled free, a piece of shell sticking to his bottom like a diaper. Its wet feathers made it look like a porcupine body with spindly legs and a long neck. In the heat of the lamp, the newly hatched chick dried, its feathers fluffing out.

Aware of Burke close beside her, Blaire couldn't help giving him a smile of delight. His answering grin warmed her, making her long to always share such moments with him. His green eyes glowed with warmth and humor. She almost felt a sense of tenderness and concern for her coming from him.

"Do you think I could hold the baby?" She whispered, as if it wouldn't be right to speak loudly in the presence of new life.

"Here, I'll pick him up for you." Burke cradled the small bird and placed it in her cupped palms. The outer feathers prickled. The ostrich looked at Blaire, its long curled eyelashes accentuating the big eyes. Blaire felt her heart melt as she contemplated this miracle of new life.

"Enjoy holding him now," Burke said. "You won't be able to hold this baby for long. Within six months he'll be taller than me."

Blaire shook her head. "It's hard to imagine they can grow that fast." Suddenly, she remembered she wouldn't be here in six months. "I don't want to get attached to these birds." Blaire held the baby toward Burke. "Here, take it back."

The door to the hatching room opened. Isabel peeked in. "You've got a visitor, Blaire."

"Another one?" Blaire gaped, pulling the small, warm, moist bird close to her again.

A tall, broad-shouldered man stepped into the room, looking out of place in a pair of their sandals. His jeans, denim shirt, and deep tan spoke of outdoor work. Light brown hair sprinkled liberally with gray peeked out from under a cowboy hat. His features looked somehow familiar, but Blaire knew she hadn't met him before.

Burke and Blaire stood at the same time. "Hey, Dad." Burke held out his hand to the man. Blaire gaped open-mouthed from one to the other. No wonder the man looked familiar. He was an older version of Burke except for his light brown eyes.

Burke turned to Blaire. "Blaire, I'd like you to meet my dad, Jed Dunham. He owns the cattle ranch that borders yours. He and Ike were good friends."

Jed smiled, his leathery face crinkling. "I'm sorry to be so long getting over here, Miss Mackenzie. I've had quite a bit to do." He held out a hand toward Blaire.

Blaire balanced the warm ostrich chick on one hand and

reached out to shake hands. As Jed Dunham's hand closed over hers, she realized her mistake. Shock registered on his face as his eyes dropped to their linked hands.

Blaire pulled her hand away, willing the bird dropping on her hand to disappear. The quiet room, once cozy, now felt suffocating. She looked up at the stern rancher contemplating the goo smeared between his fingers. "Well, at least we know his parts are working." The words popped out before she thought. Blaire could feel the red-hot blush spreading over her face.

At her side Burke burst into laughter.

# five

A few days later, Blaire followed Isabel into church. They were running late, and the swell of voices lifted in a familiar hymn drifted out to them. Burke walked close behind Blaire, but Manuel had hurried ahead to find a seat with his friends.

Blaire had visited this church two times, and she wasn't at all sure she liked it. In Chicago, she'd found anonymity in a large congregation. Here everyone knew everyone else. Oh, they were friendly enough, smiling and nodding at her as she walked through the door, greeting her with hugs and handshakes when she arrived early enough. Blaire had discovered that even though she loved crowds, she wasn't sure how comfortable she could be in such personal relationships with other Christians. For the first time, she felt expected to share her life and faith with people outside her family.

Blaire's stomach roiled as various members turned to look or gave discreet waves of their hands. At her home church she rarely shared eye contact with anyone. The people gathered for the worship service and didn't greet anyone other than the members of their small group of family or friends. The first time she'd attended church with Isabel, however, people had asked about her life history before she'd had the chance to sit down.

An older couple smiled and edged to one side, making room as Isabel moved into the pew, followed by Blaire. Burke sidled in beside her, filling the pew to capacity. His shoulder brushed against Blaire's as he reached for a hymnal. Blaire's hand grazed his as she reached to support one side of the book. She gripped the back of the pew in front of her with her left hand, feeling the padding squish stiffly beneath her fingers.

The singing ended, and Blaire sank to the pew, wedged between Isabel and Burke. She forced herself not to lean into Isabel in an effort to avoid contact with Burke. What made her so aware of this man? Even his regular breathing matched her rhythm. Burke shifted and moved his arm to rest along the back of the pew behind Blaire's shoulders. The change didn't help. Instead, the muscles along Blaire's back tensed. She wondered what it would be like to lean a little to the right, resting against Burke's side while his fingers trailed down along her shoulder. She gave herself a mental shake and opened her Bible to the Psalms as the pastor directed, praying for the ability to focus.

The pastor's deep voice filled the sanctuary. " 'The Lord is my shepherd, I shall not want. He maketh me to lie down in green pastures. . . .' " His even bass tones rolled over Blaire. She felt herself relax, the tension washing out of her.

Pastor Walker paused, taking the time to look out over the congregation. He leaned forward, his fingers curled around the edge of the podium. "For the last two weeks we've discussed the first verse of Psalm twenty-three." He grinned. "I'm sure you all have perfect recall of my messages on the Lord being our shepherd or caretaker and how we want for nothing because of that." A ripple of merriment passed over the room. Pastor Walker grinned. "Today, I want to talk about green pastures." He released the podium and stepped to the side.

"How many of you grew up where the winters were fierce?" A small showing of hands waved in the air. "I grew up in Wyoming. We had frigid winters I thought would never end." He hugged his arms around his middle. "But although the winters were long, hard, and dreary, I remember the excitement and anticipation of spring." He gestured to an older man seated toward the front of the church. "Paul,

I know you lived in the Northeast. Do you recall the color of the first green of spring?" A faint smile dimpled Paul's cheeks, and he nodded.

Pastor Walker stepped down off the dais. "I'll never forget the wonder that special color of green brought each year. I wanted to touch each blade of grass. As the pastures became covered in green, I would often lie on my back, watching the clouds overhead, smelling the damp earth, completely content. Did any of you do that?" Several heads nodded.

He stepped back up behind the podium and stared down at his Bible. " 'He maketh me to lie down in green pastures.' He maketh me." Pastor Walker's piercing gaze seemed to rest on each person for a moment as his gaze swept the room. "Why do you suppose God has to make us lie down in green pastures? Wouldn't we want to be there? Don't you think we would anticipate God's green pastures like we waited for the first green of spring?" He paused. " 'He maketh me. . . .' " He shook his head and was silent for a moment.

Blaire leaned forward, hanging onto his every word.

In words so soft the whole congregation seemed to lean closer to hear, Pastor Walker continued. "What if God doesn't see the color green in the same manner we do?" Silence stretched across the crowd. "What if our idea of green pastures is totally different from the one God truly means for us? What then? Has God made a mistake and put us in the wrong place?" Blaire felt as if the pastor were looking into her soul. "Maybe God has placed you in just the green pasture He wants you in, but you keep looking at Joe's or Mary's pasture and thinking that's where God wants you. Maybe it's time you considered that perhaps God has you right where He wants you."

Blaire's stomach clenched. She considered leaving the sanctuary, but she didn't want to make a scene. How could he say that? Why would God want her here in this barren wasteland? She knew He wouldn't do that to her.

⋅⋗⋅

Burke glared down at the open Bible in his lap. His thumb beat a silent tattoo on the edge of the pew. This sermon was precisely why he didn't come to church often. He'd only come the last few Sundays because he'd wanted to make Blaire feel at home in the community. Who did this pastor think he was? Why did he think he knew God's thoughts? Couldn't pastors be as wrong as anyone else?

As if in answer to Burke's unspoken questions, Pastor Walker said, "I don't want you to take my word on this. Check out the Scriptures, and see what pastures God placed some of His children in. Abraham had to leave his home and family and move to a strange land; the Israelites wandered in the desert for forty years; Jesus was born in a cave used to house animals." He walked down off the dais again. "Look at the prophets; look at Job—he lost all his wealth and most of his family. Look at the disciples and the hardships they endured. Are we any better, that we should expect to live in comfortable luxury, basking in the feel of a perfect pasture of our own making? No, I don't believe so. God has a purpose for each of us. He has a work for you to do, and He will place you in the right pasture so that you can accomplish His purpose."

The pastor lifted his hand, sweeping it across the crowd. "Don't try to escape the green pasture God has for you simply because the smell isn't quite what you expected or the view of the clouds isn't as clear. Ask God what His purpose is for you, then follow Him."

Burke's feet twitched with the desire to leave. It took every bit of control he possessed to stay in his seat. Why would a God who cared take away a little boy's mother, then his grandmother? That couldn't have been God's intention for his life. Granted, his grandmother had been older, and her death wasn't that odd, but what about his mother? She'd been young and vibrant, full of life. Would a loving God let a little boy grow up with only an authoritarian father who didn't have time for him? Although he and his father got along now, Burke remembered plenty of times when he'd wondered if his father would let him live to be an adult.

"In closing," the pastor said, "I want to remind you of God's love for you. He hasn't put you in a difficult pasture to punish you. He wants the best for you. He knows what's best. Trust Him."

Burke stood with the rest of the congregation. His fingers gripped the edge of the pew in front of him, and he didn't share the hymnal with Blaire for the final song. Instead, his feet were already easing toward the aisle, ready to leave this place as soon as possible.

❧

With the taste of hot sauce from lunch still warming her tongue, Blaire snuggled into an overstuffed armchair and pulled out her cross-stitch. Manuel had gone home with a friend, and she could hear Isabel puttering around in the kitchen. Burke lay in a recliner, and from the sound of his deep breathing, he was either asleep or nearly asleep. He should be tired. It had taken her several minutes to get outside after church. All the people who hadn't found out her complete history the previous Sundays were in line to get it this morning. She chuckled. They were a well-meaning group.

When she and Isabel stepped out into the warm sunshine, the first thing Blaire saw was Burke being chased by a crowd of youngsters. Girls and boys ran after him across the green churchyard. After a mad chase, Burke whirled, crouched down, and growled as he lifted one squealing child after another and swung them around like miniature airplanes. He pretended to be mad, but from their expressions, Blaire knew not one child was fooled. She shook her head. She couldn't imagine Richard ever doing something so impromptu or playful. His reserved manner would never allow such behavior.

"What are you making, *Mija?*"

Blaire started as Isabel's soft voice sounded close beside her. Did everyone in this house sneak up on people? She sighed. At least she hadn't shrieked and thrown something.

"I'm working on a cross-stitch picture." She held it up for Isabel to see. "My mother knows I like giraffes and cross-stitch so she gave this kit to me for my birthday."

"It's beautiful." Isabel held the picture to the light, then peered at the pattern in Blaire's lap. "I don't think I've ever seen such an intricate pattern. Isn't it hard to keep the count right?"

Blaire shook her head. "I've had lots of practice. Counting is one thing I am good at. After all, I'm an accountant." She grinned. "And the only klutzy thing I can do with this is drop it on occasion or poke myself with the needle."

A chuckle drifted out of the recliner across the room. Blaire thought about sailing the hoop like a Frisbee right at Burke's head but decided that with her luck she would hit the lamp behind him instead. However, she did wrinkle her nose at him when his closed eyes would not see.

"You should have Isabel show you her quilts." Burke's sleep-laden voice held a hint of laughter. "I'll bet you've never seen anything like them."

"You make quilts?" Blaire couldn't keep the astonishment from her voice. "I thought that was mostly a Midwestern art form."

Isabel blushed. "My great-grandmother learned from a pioneer woman many years ago. She was fascinated by the woman's blankets, but my great-grandmother did them a little differently. Rather than make the patterns with small pieces of material, she wanted to make her blankets a picture of life as we know it. She handed down that tradition."

"Then you learned how to quilt from your mother?"

A flicker of sadness crossed Isabel's face. "No, *Mija*. My mother died when I was very young. I do remember her quilting, but I'm not sure if it is my own memory or the one planted there by my grandmother. Grandmother is the one who taught me to quilt. She also taught me to look at the world I live in and capture that picture on the cloth."

"May I see one?" Blaire began to put away her stitchery. "I can't imagine what you're talking about. The only quilts I've seen are ones where small pieces of material are stitched together to make a pattern or one big piece of material is sewn in such a way that a design is etched into it."

"Show her the one of Ike's ranch." Burke lifted his hands behind his head and scooted the recliner out another notch.

In a few moments, Isabel returned with a large cloth bundle wrapped in plastic. Blaire leaped to help her unwrap the quilt.

"I'm afraid this one is rather large." Isabel sounded almost apologetic. "If you take the bottom and move back that way, we can stretch it out and lay it on the floor for you to look at."

Blaire tugged the edge of the quilt and backed away. She gasped in wonder as the scene unfolded on the heavy blanket. Appliquéd on a cream background was a beautiful, vivid picture of the ranch house. Ostriches stretched their necks over the edge of the fence in the background, a hen with her chicks scratched at the ground searching for food, kittens tumbled over one another in abandoned play. The quilt was alive with everyday scenes.

"Isabel, this isn't a quilt—it's a work of art. You should have it hanging in a museum somewhere." Blaire took another step back. She pulled the heavy blanket open more. She leaned back and started to take another step away.

"Be careful, *Mija!*"

Isabel's warning came too late. The back of Blaire's knee

knocked against the corner of the recliner. She stumbled back. She tried to brace herself, but her foot slipped. With a cry she tumbled into the soft chair, landing atop Burke. The air whooshed out of him. She froze, her hand still gripping the edge of the quilt.

Burke's arms came down from behind his head. He tugged her to one side. "I'm glad you brought the blanket. I was getting a little cold."

Blaire thought her face would be permanently stained flame-red.

# six

Burke ignored the amused look on Isabel's face. For the moment he reveled in how right it felt to have Blaire next to him, his arms wrapped around her. He knew he should have cautioned her about getting too close to his chair, but he hadn't. Something deep inside wanted her to get closer. For the last hour he'd pretended to sleep while he watched her. He couldn't get enough of the expressions that chased one another across her delicate features. He loved the way she bit her lower lip in concentration as she counted a section of her needlework. He'd never seen such childlike joy as she'd shown when she first glimpsed Isabel's quilt. She was just like he'd always pictured her from Ike's descriptions.

His arms tightened. For a moment he almost thought he felt Blaire snuggle in a little closer to him. Then she pushed away and began to try to get out of the chair. It wasn't easy. How he wanted to pull her back, to keep her next to him. He wanted to run his fingers through her silky hair. The faint aroma of strawberry-scented shampoo tickled his nose.

Blaire swung her legs farther to the side, trying to get up. *She's leaving as soon as she can.* The thought jolted Burke. Why did he want to hold onto her when all she planned to do was leave this place as soon as she could? He slipped his hands behind her back to help her out of the chair, but his annoyance added strength to his push. Blaire flew out of the chair and landed with a thump on the carpet.

Swinging the chair into an upright position, Burke jumped up. "I'm sorry. I meant to help you out. I didn't mean to throw you halfway across the room."

"At least between the carpet and myself there was enough padding to keep it from hurting much." Blaire grinned. "I'm not sure you fared as well when I landed on you. Sorry about that."

Burke reached down to give her a hand up. "No problem." He patted his stomach. "All these well-honed muscles kept you from doing any damage."

Isabel snorted. Blaire and Burke burst into laughter.

"Let me help you with the quilt." Burke picked up the edge Blaire had dropped. "I have to agree with Blaire, Isabel. You should consider putting some of your quilts on display at the Center for the Arts up in Globe. Their purpose is to show local artists' work."

Isabel blushed. "I'm not an artist."

"You're an artist in the same sense as one who paints a picture or makes pottery." Blaire ran a hand over the fine-stitched quilt. "This is so beautiful, you should share it with others rather than keep it wrapped in plastic."

Isabel shook her head. "I'll think about it, but I can't see why anyone would want to look at these hanging on a wall. Now, why don't you help me fold this quilt? Then you two can go for a walk, and I'll start some supper."

Burke glanced at Blaire. Bright blue eyes gazed back at him. He lifted his eyebrows in a question. She smiled.

"That sounds like a good idea, Isabel. Maybe I can introduce Blaire to some of the plant life around here."

❧

Early the next morning, Blaire stretched and wiggled down into the embracing softness of the bed as golden sunlight streamed through the slit in the blinds covering her bedroom window. She wanted to sleep longer. She felt like staying in bed all morning and doing nothing.

"Lord, I'm getting lazy. I can't remember when I've slept in so much on a work day. Help me to find a purpose here."

Blaire closed her eyes. A picture of Burke, the edges of his eyes crinkled with laughter, flashed across her vision. "Lord, help me get away from this place before I don't want to leave. I need to get back to the city." She sighed and threw back the covers. "For now, just show me a purpose for my life, please."

A half hour later, freshly showered, Blaire headed for the kitchen. "Mmm, Isabel. I don't know how one person can make so many different delicious smells come from the same oven. You must spend all your time cooking."

"I would like that, *Mija*." Isabel set a steaming plate of food on the table. "Since your uncle Ike died, we have had many chores to do."

Blaire sat down and looked up into Isabel's dark eyes. "What do you do besides the cooking and housework? I thought Burke and Manuel did all the outside chores."

"They do all the heavy work—feeding the ostriches, moving them when it's needed, and taking care of the processing plant. But someone has to watch over the eggs and the new hatchlings. I also take care of the little garden we have. We all like fresh vegetables, especially those hot peppers you love."

Blaire grimaced, remembering the first time she'd eaten a fresh jalapeño pepper. Her eyes had watered. Her nose had run. Her throat had burned all the way down. She'd drunk what seemed like six gallons of water without cooling off the burning. Then she tried a second bite, determined it couldn't be as bad as the first. She'd been right. The second bite was worse.

"Maybe you can show me how to help. I'll do anything except sample the peppers to see if they're ready." Blaire fanned herself with a hand, and Isabel laughed.

"You don't have to help. We're used to our routine."

"No, I feel a little useless. Besides, just this morning I asked the Lord to show me His purpose for my life. Maybe until I get back to the city, my purpose is to help you out. I'll go crazy if I just sit around doing nothing all day."

"Finish your breakfast, then, and we'll head out to see how the babies are doing." Isabel began to rinse off dishes and load the dishwasher as Blaire savored the spicy ranch eggs she'd been served.

Stepping out into the early morning, Blaire drew in a deep breath. "You know, I thought I would hate it here. At first everything seemed so barren and empty."

"And now?" Isabel paused, giving her a questioning look.

"I don't know. I guess the desert grows on you. The mountains are different than skyscrapers, but they're God's handiwork. Sometimes when I sit on the porch swing, I can almost picture Him molding them, like a toddler molds clay. I picture the concentration on His face and the delight once He got them shaped just right." She felt her face warm. "I suppose that sounds silly."

Isabel shook her head. "Not at all. I love to look at this country and see how God worked. Most of the plants are prickly and seem unfriendly, but they had to be that way to survive. It was part of God's design. Did you know that the Saguaro cactus roots don't go down into the ground like tree roots?" Isabel gestured at the tall cacti dotting the hills around them.

Blaire gazed up at a multi-armed cactus. "How does it get water without roots? Surely it can't live without water."

"Oh, Saguaros need water, all right. They have roots, but the roots don't go down into the ground. There isn't any water up on the hills where the cactus grows. Instead, the Saguaro's roots run in a large network parallel to the surface of the ground. Then, when we do get rain, the Saguaro can take the most advantage of the small amount of moisture."

"I see." Blaire stared in wonder at the huge cactus. "God knew they needed roots going to the side or they would die."

Isabel smiled and led the way to the hatchery. "I think that's why God puts us all in different places. He knows we all have different needs. Like the pastor said the other day, God puts us in the right green pasture. We just have to accept that."

Blaire glanced up at the cacti on the hills. Burke had explained yesterday that Saguaros only grew in a small area of the Southwest. They couldn't survive at higher elevations or in colder climates. *That is why I need to get back to the city. I could never survive out here, no matter how beautiful the country is.*

Mimicking Isabel, Blaire left her shoes at the door, donning sterile sandals and washing her hands with disinfectant soap. Burke or Manuel had already delivered the day's cache of eggs.

"Each day we have to put the new eggs in the incubator. You have to label them so we all know which eggs are which. If we get them mixed up, we'll never know who's supposed to hatch when. Burke insists on keeping good records." She gestured to a book on a table at the side of the room. "It's pretty self-explanatory. You can follow the previous entries and know what to do."

"Do you really trust a klutz like me to handle such big eggs?" Blaire chuckled. "You might end up with a floor covered in goo before I finish. The ranch could go broke."

Isabel grinned. "I suppose we've all dropped an egg on occasion. Don't worry. You'll be tossing the eggs around like a pro pretty soon."

Pulling open a door, Isabel gestured to the number at the top corner of the incubator. "We'll put today's eggs in number six. Then we have to check the other eggs and turn them."

They worked silently for several minutes. Blaire marveled at the pebbly feel of the giant eggs. As she helped turn the eggs, she wondered if she could actually feel movement inside or if her imagination was running wild.

Isabel watched as she recorded the information in the book. "Doesn't Burke keep these records in the computer?"

"Burke and computers don't get along well. I'm not sure if he doesn't like the computer or if he hasn't had the time to familiarize himself with the program. If you would like to take over the computer work while you're here, I'm sure he would love it. I know Ike had good intentions, but that man didn't understand computers at all."

"I think I was raised by a computer." Blaire grinned at the mental picture. "I'll have a look at the books later today or tomorrow. Are we done out here?"

"Oh, no. This is only the beginning. Now I have to feed the babies." Isabel's dark eyes twinkled. "The new ones are the most fun. They require special assistance."

Blaire followed Isabel into the feed shed. Isabel scooped up a can of tiny, rough, green pebbles. "What kind of feed is this?" Blaire ran her hand through the coarse, granular mass.

"These are hay crumbles, made especially for the babies. The older birds get hay pellets, similar to rabbit pellets. They're made of compressed hay."

"I never thought about what they would eat. I guess I assumed they ate bugs or something like chickens do. If we had chickens, would the baby ostriches eat the chicken feed?"

"We don't keep chickens. We had them at first, but we found out the hard way that chickens and pigs contaminate the eggs of the ostriches. We had to get rid of the chickens. I don't think they eat the same feed, but I'm not sure. You can ask Burke. He would know."

Blaire followed Isabel's example and poured feed into a feeder. Then she sprinkled some of the pellets on the ground. Isabel's pen of young ones rushed right in and began to peck at the feed. Blaire's didn't seem to know what to do.

"What's wrong with these ostriches? They won't eat."

Isabel laughed. "They need you to teach them how. These

are the new babies, and they haven't caught on yet."

"Teach them?" Blaire stared at Isabel.

"In the wild they would follow their parents' examples. Here, they don't have that example so you have to be their parent."

"How can I possibly do that? I don't even have a beak." Blaire suspected Isabel was jesting with her.

"Let me show you." Isabel eased down onto her knees in the dirt. She bent forward, her hand close to her face so that her fingers looked like a bird beak. Then she darted her face down toward the dirt as if pecking at the pellets. The baby ostriches tilted their heads to one side, watching the demonstration.

Blaire burst out laughing. "Do you really do this, or are you trying to trick the city girl into doing something silly?"

"I really do this. It's the only way to teach them that I know of." She chuckled. "But I try to do it when no one else is around."

"Okay, if you can, so can I." Blaire grabbed her hair with one hand, holding it back from her face. She folded the fingers of her other hand together, held them near her mouth, and poked at the ground. The little ostriches moved closer. Their bright eyes followed her jabbing motion. Their little heads tilted to the other side as they watched. "Come on, you guys, I'm trying to teach an important lesson here." Once more, Blaire pecked at the ground. One of the babies stretched its neck and pecked with her.

"He did it. Did you see that, Isabel?"

Isabel laughed. "You're a natural teacher, *Mija*. Maybe you should give up accounting and teach babies to eat."

Blaire grinned and went back to working with the doe-eyed ostriches.

❧

"Look here, Manuel. Those birds have been pulling at the

fence again. I'll head up to the house and get the tools we need to fix it before they break out and run on us." Burke knew that once out and running, there would be no stopping the ostriches. They were too fast and too wild to catch easily.

"I'll wait here for you. While you're gone, I'll check the rest of the fence."

Burke strode down the lane, choosing to walk the short distance rather than taking the truck. For what seemed like the hundredth time that morning, he wondered what Blaire was doing. How had that girl gotten under his skin so fast? He could still see the sun dancing on the golden highlights of her hair when they went for that walk yesterday. For someone who didn't want to stay in Arizona, she sure displayed an avid interest in the plants and animals of the area. He loved her curiosity and challenging questions.

Lost in thought, Burke didn't notice Isabel and Blaire until he was nearly on top of them. He stopped and watched Blaire as she encouraged the young birds to eat. They stared at her with comical interest, dipping their heads down when she did, as if wondering what this funny-looking bird was up to. Burke bit his lip to keep from laughing and thought about slipping away without letting Blaire and Isabel know that he'd watched. Then he remembered the tools he needed. He had to go right by the pens. He couldn't avoid Blaire.

"That's a fine new ostrich we've got there, Isabel."

## seven

Blaire's shoulders stiffened. A red flush drifted up her cheek. Burke could almost hear her wishing the ground would open up and swallow her. She released her hair, and the golden waves fell forward, a small curtain to hide behind. She pushed against the ground and straightened up, brushing the dirt from her knees. The baby ostriches heads moved as one, following her upward movement.

"I suppose you think it's fun to laugh at me." Blaire ran her fingers back through her hair, pushing it away from her face.

Burke adjusted his hat on his head. He fought a valiant battle against the humor bubbling up inside of him. "I didn't come here on purpose to spy on you. I came to get some fencing materials out of the shed." He gestured toward the medium-sized barn behind the hatchery.

"You could have made a little more noise." Blaire leaned forward, her eyes flashing fire.

Burke rubbed his jaw. "I could have just burst out laughing. That would have let you know I was here." He tried to look contrite. "Look, I'm sorry I embarrassed you. I'll try not to do it anymore."

Burke started on toward the shed.

"Wait just a minute." Blaire charged out of the pen and up to him. "I'm tired of always doing something stupid and having you catch me."

Burke stopped walking and looked down at her. "Then the solution is simple. Stop doing something stupid." A thundercloud rippled across her face. Burke lifted his hands in mock surrender and backed toward the barn door. "Now wait a minute. I was only joking. You weren't doing anything stupid. All of us have had to teach the baby ostriches to eat at one time or another."

She crossed her arms, staring hard at him.

"It could have been worse," Burke said. Blaire looked doubtful. "I could have gone in the house and gotten the video camera. Just think of the ammunition that would have been." He chuckled, then began to laugh as he backed through the door and into the barn.

"This calls for war." Blaire followed him inside. "I believe I'll follow you around secretly and see if you don't do something stupid. Maybe I'll even bring along that trusty video camera."

"If it's war you want. . ." Burke reached over her head and pulled something off a shelf. "I'll give you war." Burke flourished a long feather duster, the ostrich feathers dancing with the sudden motion.

Blaire stared as if too surprised to move. Her mouth fell open. Her eyes widened. Burke chuckled. He took up what he hoped was a fencing stance. *"En garde,* Mademoiselle." His feather duster nearly brushed her nose.

Jumping back, Blaire reached up on the shelf. She brought down a second feather duster. Her eyes took on a determined look. "This is a fight to the finish." Her twitching lips belied her solemn tone. "Surrender now, or say your prayers."

"I'll never surrender." Burke swept forward, aiming for her cheek. Blaire jumped back and parried his blow. She seemed to have a much better stance than he did. Maybe she was a swashbuckling movie fan.

Blaire twisted to the right and dusted his neck. The feathers' soft tickling made him jump. He fought hard, determined to get her back.

"You're wounded. Are you ready to surrender?" Blaire knocked aside his feather duster. Her blue eyes mocked him.

Burke barked a fake laugh. "Ha! Mademoiselle, I believe you were the one who set the rules. This is a fight to the death."

Blaire's feather duster whipped in with surprising speed. Burke felt his hat flying through the air.

"Now, you're getting serious." He swivelled around to face her as she dodged and parried. "That was a mortal wound to my favorite hat. No one messes with my hat and lives."

"You don't seem to have the room to talk. So far you haven't landed a single blow." Blaire's flushed face and dancing eyes took the edge off her challenge.

"In a daring move, the illustrious swordsman leaps toward his opponent. He backs her against the wall and knocks her sword from her hand." Burke jumped forward, pinning Blaire against a stack of straw bales. He grabbed her feather duster, wrenched it from her hand, and tossed it behind them. With his other hand he held down her hands.

"Now the swordsman must decide. Is it death, or will he show mercy?" Burke tried to hold back his laughter. "He decides. No mercy."

The feather duster began a dance over Blaire's cheeks, arms, and neck. She giggled, trying to jerk away as the soft feathers tickled her. "Stop that. I surrender. I surrender."

"That won't work." Burke continued to tickle. "We agreed to fight to the death."

Blaire tried to step around him, but her foot slipped in the loose straw. Seeing her start to fall, Burke grabbed her, pulling her close to him. He looked down into those sky blue eyes. Time stood still. He held his breath. Blaire didn't move. The laughter stopped.

"The swordsman demands a penance. A kiss for her life." At Burke's soft whisper, Blaire's eyes widened. The kiss was sweet, drawing him in, making him long for more. The feather duster clattered to the ground. Burke released Blaire and stepped back. He knew for once his was the reddest face.

"I'm sorry. Manuel and I fence sometimes. I got carried away." He picked up his hat and shoved it back on his head.

"I'm hoping you require a different penance from Manuel when you beat him." Blaire's lips twitched, as if she wanted to smile but couldn't. Her voice had a slight quaver. She edged past him and almost ran toward the house.

Burke picked up the feather dusters and put them back on the shelf. What had come over him? Why did Blaire make him act this way? She was feisty and playful at the same time. Seeing her out there with her hands on her hips, staring him down, he'd wanted to grab her and kiss her. She challenged him. She was such a mixture of fun and serious, and he was never sure which one would show up next. Rather than confusing him, she was refreshing. Besides, he'd never met a woman so willing to laugh at herself.

Then when she'd followed him in here, he had no idea what had possessed him to start a fencing battle. Yet she played right along. He couldn't remember having such a good time with anyone else. Something changed, though. When he caught her in his arms, she felt like she belonged there. Their kiss felt right too. He felt as if God placed her there just for him. He found himself wanting to get to know her. He wanted to get to know her in a way that would take a lifetime to complete. Burke rubbed the back of his neck. What was happening to him? Of all the women to be attracted to, he had to pick one who wouldn't be staying around long. He grabbed up the materials he needed and headed out of the barn. Maybe that was best. If Blaire left soon, then he could forget her. Because he sure couldn't seem to get her off his mind while she was here.

❧

Blaire rolled down the window as she drove toward town. The spring air felt good circling through the car. Maybe the breeze would chase away the turmoil of thoughts and images in her mind. Her lips still felt the kiss Burke had placed there moments before. This wasn't right. He worked for her. Hadn't she learned anything from her disastrous relationship with Richard? "You shouldn't date someone you work with. You shouldn't date someone you work with." Her hand pounded the rhythm of her words on the steering wheel as she spouted the litany.

When she'd run toward the house, she'd known she'd have to leave the ranch for awhile. Cleaning up, she'd grabbed some letters she'd written to her family and asked Isabel for directions to the nearest post office. The road wound through a canyon. On one side, steep cliffs rose perpendicular to the road. On the other side, the canyon dropped off to the floor where the Gila River followed its twisting path. Her uncle Ike's car, now hers, handled the highway's curves like a dream.

Above the cliffs in front of her, Blaire spotted the tall smokestack of the town's copper mine. A few minutes later she turned on the highway that ran through the center of town. The post office was two blocks into town, right where Isabel had said it would be. In a town this size, Blaire wondered how anyone could ever get lost.

"I'd like a book of stamps, please." Blaire smiled at the clerk. Her bluish white beehive hairdo made Blaire want to poke and prod to see what was hidden in those depths. How could anyone have that much hair?

"There's your change, Dear." Spots of rouge brightened the woman's cheeks.

"Thank you." Blaire slipped the change in her purse and started to leave. She turned back. "Excuse me. Can you tell me if there's a real estate agent in town?"

The woman laughed. "Land sakes, no. We don't have much business here since one of the copper mines closed down. Too many people moved away. I believe there's a

Realtor in Kearny, though."

"Is that very far?"

"I can tell you aren't from around here." The woman patted her impossibly high hair. "Kearny is about eleven miles that way." She pointed down the highway that ran through town. "You can't miss it. Are you looking for some property to buy?"

"No, I'm looking to sell." Blaire hesitated, knowing whatever she said would probably be around town before long. What did it matter? Maybe the news would reach some buyer before she even listed the ranch. "I inherited my uncle's ranch. It's north of town. Ike Mackenzie's place."

"Oh, yes." The woman's eyes sparkled. "I've heard about you coming to town, Miss Mackenzie. That Ike was quite a character." She nudged her hair and blushed. Lowering her voice, she leaned across the counter. "I think he might have been sweet on me. He sure was one for the flattery."

Blaire smiled at the revelation of a side of her uncle she'd never seen. He'd always had a way with words, but she couldn't imagine him being a flirt. As she walked toward her car, she wondered if sometimes women, and men too, read more into bantering than was meant. Had Burke thought she was flirting with him today? Was that why he'd kissed her?

She made the short drive to Kearny, nearly missing the small town nestled among the hills. Turning off the highway, she found the main street. After cruising up and down a few minutes, she stopped and asked for directions. In a few minutes she'd stopped outside Valley Realty. A scribbled sign taped to the door announced, "Be back in an hour." No time was given. Had the agent just left, or had they been gone for almost an hour? Blaire decided she didn't want to wait. She wasn't sure she wanted to list her property with someone that irresponsible.

The drive home took less than half an hour. The late

afternoon sky turned an azure blue. Not a cloud darkened the horizon. For the first time, Blaire began to understand how such openness could give a person a sense of freedom. "Lord, I think I need to find a shopping mall. I'm in danger of singing a song about cows and open spaces. I need a couple of skyscrapers or at least a building with more than one story."

Back home, Blaire felt a restlessness she couldn't explain. She heard Isabel puttering in the kitchen. Not feeling like company, Blaire headed for her room. She picked up her cross-stitch and put it back down. She wandered around looking at her giraffes and the pictures of her family.

She plunked down on the edge of the bed. The waterbed moved gently, then stopped. Her Bible sat on the table by her bed. Blaire picked it up, rolled over onto her stomach, and stretched out across the bed to read. Thinking of the pastor's message from the previous Sunday, she turned to Psalm 23.

" 'The Lord is my Shepherd, I shall not want.' " She spoke the words softly, then stopped to think about them. "Yes, Lord, You are my shepherd. I gave You my life to do with as You see fit." She ran her hand over the smooth page. "So why do I feel like You're not in charge? Am I still trying to run my life? I thought I knew what You wanted for me. You brought me here, but I'm an accountant. I can't possibly do my job from here. I know nothing about running an ostrich ranch, so what do You want me to do? Can't You send me something in black and white? I'm willing to follow. I just don't know where to go. Lord, help me."

Tears blurred the fine print in front of her. Was she too concerned with her wants to see where the Lord was leading? "Lord, I don't know what I want. I only know I can't stand the thought of being hurt again. Protect me from Burke, Lord. I have to stay away from him. Help me sell this ranch so I can leave here before I find myself doing something I'll regret."

She thought of her relationship with Richard. Her feelings

for him had never been love, but she'd been too blind to see. He was the boss's son. Every girl in the office wanted him to notice her. When he'd asked her out, Blaire had known that all the other girls were jealous. It had been a heady feeling. She could hear her mom once more saying, *"Pride goeth before destruction."* Mom was right. She hadn't loved Richard. She'd used him as much as he'd used her.

"Thank You, Lord, for keeping me from making such a terrible mistake with my life." She and Richard had little in common. They'd never laughed together. They'd rarely talked of anything other than work or upcoming wedding plans.

Her thoughts turned to Burke. She could see his smile. He made her want to smile. He made her laugh. When she pulled a klutz move, as her family called it, Burke laughed with her rather than getting angry as Richard had done. Burke could be a wonderful friend. He was comfortable. They had so much in common. "Lord, I need to leave now. He's too dangerous. I don't want to lose my heart to him."

# eight

The loud squeak of a chair wheel and the slam of a drawer woke Blaire early the next morning. She snuggled deeper into the covers and glanced at the clock. What awful hour was this anyway? She bolted upright in bed. Leaning closer to the night table, she gasped. Eight-thirty! She'd slept until eight-thirty in the morning? She wanted to slide down in the bed in embarrassment. She hadn't slept this late since she'd had the flu last winter.

She swung her legs over the side of the bed. "So much for country air being healthy. I thought I would rise at the crack of dawn, able to work long hours without tiring, and eating like a horse without gaining weight. Now I find I can't even get to sleep at night."

The chair in the office creaked again. Blaire stopped her soliloquy. She had better be careful. If she could hear the chair, chances were good that the person in the other room could hear her talking. The sudden click of the door leading to the office answered her question. Whoever was in there must have realized she was awake.

"Please don't let it have been Burke." Even as she whispered her plea, she knew Burke was the only suspect. Isabel had already admitted that she didn't have anything to do with the computer, and Manuel mostly did the outside chores. Blaire recalled another time she'd heard the squeak of that chair. Burke must have heard her tell Isabel about Richard. In a way she felt relieved that he knew.

Burke had no way of knowing he was the reason she was so tired this morning. She'd tossed and turned all night thinking of his kiss, the need to sell the ranch, and wondering where God's green pasture for her could be located.

Blaire decided not to shower. She didn't feel comfortable with someone so close to her bathroom. This setup with the office sharing a bathroom with the master bedroom had been fine when her uncle was the one doing the office work and using the bedroom. As the situation stood now, however, she didn't appreciate someone else having such easy access to her room.

She slipped on a teal blue blouse, whose color was reflected in a scene-from-Africa skirt. Zebras and giraffes paraded in relief across a black background. Her sister and brother-in-law had sent the skirt to her for her last birthday. She missed her sister, Clarissa. They had been so close. She always wore something from Clarissa when she needed to talk to her sister. For some reason wearing something her sister had picked out for her helped ease the lonely ache.

The kitchen was empty when Blaire got there, and she assumed Isabel was out working in the hatchery. A bowl of fresh fruit stood in the middle of the dining table. A note from Isabel told her there were eggs in the refrigerator, cereal in the cupboards, and bagels in the bread drawer.

"So you finally decided to get up."

Blaire grabbed the counter to keep herself from jumping. She would not give Burke the satisfaction of knowing he'd startled her again. She turned. "I had a little trouble sleeping last night. I guess I decided to make up for it this morning." Blaire noticed that Burke's eyes looked a little drawn. Had he missed some sleep too?

Burke nodded and leaned against the doorjamb. "I wondered if you could give me some help when you've had your breakfast."

"Me?"

"Sure. I need someone to wrestle a couple of those big male ostriches for me." Sea green eyes sparkled with mischief.

"Oops. I forgot to put on my wrestling clothes. Besides, I'm more the fencing type than the wrestling type." The reference to yesterday's mock sword play slipped out. Blaire felt her face flame as she thought of the way the incident had ended. Her heart pounded. How could she still be so aware of Burke's closeness?

"Actually, I had hoped you might have your accountant clothes on. We had a big order in yesterday's mail. I'm still struggling with the way Ike set up the books."

Blaire pushed off from the counter. "You ordered an accountant?" She lifted her hand to her brow in a mock salute. "Here I am, front and center, Sir."

"This branch of the service may be tough, but I will let you have some breakfast before you report for duty."

"One breakfast coming up." Blaire grabbed an apple from the bowl on the table. She tossed the piece of fruit up in the air. Burke cringed. With a snap, she caught the sweet missile in her right hand. "Ha! You didn't think me capable of doing anything remotely coordinated, did you?"

"You wound me, my lady." Burke staggered back, his hand covering his heart. "In my eyes you are the epitome of grace."

Blaire narrowed her eyes and waved her apple in his face. "You don't fool me. You're only saying that because you need help with the books."

Burke plucked the apple from her hand and took a big bite. "You're absolutely right. Get yourself another apple and follow me, Grace."

Laughter bubbled up inside her. Blaire chose a banana and trailed after Burke to the office. At his questioning look she said, "I wanted to be a fruit of a different color. Two of a kind might be too much."

❧

Burke pulled a second chair up to the computer. He considered kicking himself while he was at it. He'd spent a good portion of the night thinking about Blaire and how he needed to keep his distance. Then, the first time he saw her, he started in with the light-hearted banter. *Why do I do this?* Almost before he asked the question he knew the answer. Because she was so much fun to talk to and to tease. He couldn't ever remember feeling this way about another woman.

"I don't know how familiar you are with computers. Not long before he died, Ike had this one installed. He wanted to put all of the business records on the computer to keep better track of everything. I'm not sure he understood the machine, and I'm not good with these types of programs. I get lost every time I try to figure out what he was doing."

"What records did he want to keep track of?" Blaire leaned closer to the screen, scanning the various file names.

"Let's see." Burke leaned back in his chair and held up his hand, ticking the items off on his fingers. "There's egg production, the breeder program, egg sales, meat and leather sales, feather sales, and the sale and raising of our juveniles and early breeders." He frowned. Blaire was staring at him. "I think that's all."

"I had no idea so much was involved." She glanced at the screen, then back at him. "What do you want to try to look up first?"

"Let's try the juveniles and early breeders. The order form says this guy wants to buy twenty-four breeder hens, eight male breeders, and several juveniles."

"I thought you said this was a big order." Blaire's eyebrows drew together. She picked up a pencil and tapped it on the desk. "What do these ostriches cost, two to three hundred apiece? That doesn't seem like so much to me."

Burke tried to close his mouth. He knew he probably looked stupid with it hanging open. "Didn't the lawyers in Phoenix go over this with you?" He took a deep breath and tried to stop spluttering. "Do you mean you have no idea of the value of this ranch, your inheritance?"

Puzzled blue eyes met his. Blaire shrugged. "I don't think I gave the lawyers time to tell me much. They gave me a bunch of paperwork, but I haven't looked at it yet. Can you explain the value to me?"

Taking a last bite of apple, Burke stepped into the bathroom to wash the sticky juice from his hand. When she found out the real worth of this enterprise, would Blaire be even more eager to sell the ranch? He took a deep sigh and headed back into the office. He couldn't hide the truth.

"Your uncle Ike wanted to raise the best ostriches. He spent several years doing other things while he studied the markets and earned some starting money. He found out that the best birds are the South African black ostriches. He looked at different breeding stock until he found just the right line. That's what he bought. You have the best birds possible on this ranch. We don't just raise ostriches. We raise the cream of the crop, so to speak."

"I didn't even know there were different kinds of ostriches. What's so special about these black ones?"

"The African blacks have about twenty percent more feathers, and their hides are worth more than any other ostrich. Seventy percent of the value of the bird is in the skin and feathers."

"Poor things." Blaire swept her hair back from her face. "Is that all we raise them for?"

"They're like cows. You eat a hamburger and don't think about the cute little cow when you bite into that sandwich."

Blaire nodded. "I guess you're right. But I haven't just taught a baby cow to peck food in the dirt either."

Burke chuckled. "That's a good thing. A calf would look pretty stupid pecking in the dirt."

Blaire flipped the pencil at him. "So, how much does an ostrich cost?"

"That depends on the ostrich, its age, and whether the bird is for breeding or other purposes."

"Are you avoiding my question? I mean, how could a stupid bird be as valuable as a cow? There's something un-American about that."

Burke leaned back in the chair. "Now you sound like my dad and all the other cattle ranchers I know. They think ostriches are trying to steal their market away from them by appealing to health nuts."

Blaire twisted a hank of hair between her fingers. A frown wrinkled her brow. "Okay, I'll bite. What do health nuts have to do with ostriches?"

"Ostrich meat is lower in fat than even venison and higher in iron than beef. Beef and pork have more than nine grams of fat, and ostrich meat has less than three grams. For people looking to decrease their fat intake, this meat is a viable alternative." He grinned. "How's that for a commercial?"

"Okay, Smartie, what about chicken or turkey? They're birds, and they're lower in fat than beef or pork." She leaned back and pointed her pencil at him. "And they're much easier to get in the oven."

"Too bad. You'll have to get a bigger oven. Skinned chicken has more than seven grams of fat, and turkey without the skin has five." He put his hand to his ear. "Hark, is that a group of health nuts at the door?"

They both laughed.

"I think we got off track." Burke pointed at the computer screen. "If you look in the breeder file, I'll show you a little of what ostriches are worth. I think that's the only file Ike had done much work on."

Blaire clicked on the filename and watched a column of figures pop up on the screen. She gasped and turned to Burke, her eyes wide. "These figures can't be right."

"Not all ostriches are worth this much. I told you Ike

studied the market and picked his birds from the best. These are the birds we've set aside to sell as breeders. The younger ones sell for twenty-eight hundred dollars each, and the older ones sell for thirty-eight hundred each. We have between two hundred and two hundred and fifty of each age group set aside to sell this season. The buyer said in his E-mail this morning that he wants twenty of the younger breeders and twelve of the older ones."

Burke reached over and put his finger on Blaire's chin. He pushed up gently and chuckled. "You're going to catch flies that way." She didn't say anything, just stared at him. "You really didn't know how much this place is worth, did you?"

She shook her head, staring at him. A deep breath shuddered through her. "Do you realize those five hundred birds you're talking about will bring in more than a million dollars if they all sell? Just the one sale we're talking about will bring in more than a hundred thousand dollars. Where did Uncle Ike get the money to start the ranch? I had no idea he could afford something of this magnitude."

"He made some investments that paid off. Also, he put every penny he made back into building the stock. He worked hard to get this ranch going. You have inherited a business worth several million dollars. Ike talked a lot about how he wanted to have you come out here and help him with the ranch. He said your accounting skills would be put to good use."

"He invited me out here, but he didn't say anything about wanting me to work for him."

"I think he wanted you to see the place first. Ike thought you would be a natural here. He said you were always a good one to look for a new experience. Maybe that's why he liked you so much. You two had a lot in common."

Blaire leaned forward, studying the open file intently. Burke could almost see her mathematical training taking over. The columns of figures that were Greek to him obviously made sense to her. She clicked the file closed and opened another. There wasn't much to see in it. Ike had only begun to keep records on the computer, and the other files were mostly empty.

What would she do now? Would she be even more eager to sell the ranch? She could take the money and open her own accounting firm as she had mentioned. Or would she see what Ike wanted to do here and continue his dream? Burke hoped she would choose the latter, but she hadn't seemed eager to stay so far.

"Where did Ike keep his figures before he used the computer?" Blaire's blue gaze flicked to him before going back to the screen.

"In the books in this drawer." Burke opened a drawer at the side of the desk. "I think he kept pretty accurate records." He reached to pick up a book at the same time as Blaire. His hand closed over hers. Awareness of her made him pause. He looked up. Eyes wide, she had focused her full attention on him. Burke tried to think of something to say that would lighten the moment, but he could barely breathe, let alone think.

# nine

The touch of the book's cool binding under Blaire's fingers contrasted sharply with the warm tingling sensation of Burke's hand on hers. Blaire looked into his green eyes. For once, he wasn't teasing. No laughter crinkled the corners of his eyes. Instead, a look of longing tugged at her heart. *I was right.* The words echoed inside her head. *He is dangerous. He's stealing my heart. I have to learn all there is about this ranch, then sell the place.*

Dragging her gaze from Burke's, Blaire pulled the book from the drawer. Burke let go, then sat back, releasing a long breath.

"I think I'll give you some time to look over the books. I'll stop back in later and discuss the buyer with you." He pushed back his chair and stood. She watched him slip his hat back on his head. "Do you have any other questions before I go? I think Ike left most everything in the desk somewhere."

Blaire glanced at the large oak desk. There were several account books in the open drawer. "I'll find what I need. You can go ahead with whatever you have to be doing." As he left, Blaire forced herself to ignore his retreating back. Instead, she immersed herself in the columns of figures, something that never failed to grab her complete attention. The world faded as she concentrated on the work in front of her.

A hand squeezed Blaire's shoulder. She jumped. The book on the desk slipped to the floor. The bang echoed in the small room. She whirled around. Burke grinned down at her.

"I've heard of people getting into their work, but you're amazing."

She felt her face flush. "The next time you might try calling my name."

"How many times?"

"What do you mean?"

"Well, let's see." He tilted his head back as if thinking and rubbed his jaw with his fingers. "I called through the window, I called from out in the living room where I stopped to talk to Isabel. Then I said your name twice in here before I touched you." He looked down at her again. "So, how often should I call you?"

Blaire pursed her lips. She could remember all the times she had been accused of being on another planet when her coworkers tried to get her attention. Flipping her hair back over her shoulders, she lifted her nose in the air and sniffed like a haughty snob. "When you reach the proper number of requests to merit my response, then I will answer, but only then."

Burke laughed, the corners of his eyes crinkling. Blaire joined him.

"I have to admit my coworkers would commiserate with you. My friend Susan used to keep a little squirt gun handy. She loved to come up behind me and squirt cold water on my neck."

Burke rubbed his jaw. "Hmm. I think I may have an old squirt gun I can resurrect."

"I wouldn't if I were you." Blaire narrowed her gaze. "I haven't told you what vile deeds I did to Susan to pay her back."

"What happened to vengeance belonging to the Lord?"

Blaire chuckled. "I thought He could use some help."

Burke lifted his hat and raked his fingers through his hair. "I give up. Now, in case you're wondering why I'm interrupting you, I have something to show you out in the barn. I just made a discovery. Since you are the owner, you need to take a look."

Curious, Blaire pushed back the chair and stood up. Stiff muscles protested. She rotated her shoulders, easing a kink out of her back. "I can't imagine what you need my advice on around here. I don't know anything yet." She smirked at him. "Unless you're asking for a fencing rematch." She groaned inside. Why did she keep bringing that up? "Let's go. I do need to stretch a little."

A gentle breeze stirred the leaves of the mesquite trees. The sun's rays, accompanied by a warm breeze, caused sweat to wash over Blaire on the short walk to the barn. She watched the male ostrich in the nearest pen. He stalked around the enclosure, fanning his dark feathers as if he were the one creating a draft. The hens pecked at the ground while scrutinizing their mate as he made the rounds.

Inside the barn, Blaire stopped to let her eyes adjust to the dim light. A variety of tools lined one wall. Everything from gardening implements to incubator parts had a place. Amazed at the orderliness, she wondered if Burke or Manuel kept the place so well organized.

"Over here." Burke beckoned to one corner where a few bales of straw lined the wall. "I was in here getting an extension cord when I heard them."

"Heard what?" Blaire stopped in midstride.

"These critters." Burke leaned down, peering behind one of the bales. He stuck one hand in, and Blaire could hear faint, high-pitched mewling sounds. She eased up next to him and leaned closer. Burke pulled out his hand, his fingers curled around a tiny spitfire.

"A kitten." Blaire held out her hands. "I don't think I've ever seen one so young." The little black-and-white kitten opened its small pink mouth and hissed, trying for all the world to act fierce. Little baby fur stood on end. Blaire giggled. "If he had some size to back him up, I think he'd eat me for dinner." She stroked a finger down the shaking back.

"Hold him next to your heart." Burke demonstrated, lifting a gray-and-white kitten up and cuddling it on his chest. "I think the heartbeat helps to calm them."

Blaire followed his example. She cupped her hand under the baby to support him. In moments the kitten curled up and went to sleep. "Look at these paws." She lifted one paw with her fingertip. Minuscule pink pads housed almost clear barbs that were so soft they couldn't possibly do much damage to anything.

She looked up to find Burke watching her. His large finger slowly stroked the back of his kitten as it slept. The tender look in his eyes caught and held her. She wanted to look away but found she couldn't. She wished he would touch her with the same tenderness. The kitten in her hand moved. Breaking eye contact with Burke, she watched the matchstick legs stretch out stiff and the little mouth open in a wide yawn.

"How old are they?"

"It's hard to say." Burke held his kitten up to eye level, as if trying to read the age. "They're probably close to two weeks, but not much older. Kittens open their eyes when they're about ten days old. These have their eyes open, but they still don't have a lot of coordination. That will come in the next week or two. Then they'll start wandering away from home."

"I didn't even know we had any cats." Blaire snuggled the kitten next to her cheek for a minute before handing it to Burke to put back.

"Ike tried to get rid of cats when they came around. He didn't like them around the ostriches."

"Why would cats make a difference?"

Burke straightened. "Have you ever been around cats during their mating season?"

"I've never had one. The neighbors did, though. I remember more than once having trouble sleeping because of the caterwauling going on in the alley behind our house. Is that what you're referring to?"

"Yep. That caterwauling, as you call it, will get the ostriches so upset they won't lay eggs. They hate unusual noises. Ostriches are bothered by strange animals such as coyotes howling or even cats walking by their pen. There are a lot of coyotes in the area. We can't keep them all away, but we try to discourage them from coming around the breeding pens."

Blaire glanced out the door at the huge birds. How could a little cat bother something so big? "Will we need to get rid of the mother?"

Rubbing the back of his neck, Burke grimaced. "I hate to do that. She's a good mouser. However, I think we should give the kittens away when they're old enough. We can always take them over to Dad's place."

"He's not afraid of ending up with too many?"

Burke's green eyes twinkled. "He has a hard time keeping cats around. They always get invited to lunch with the coyotes and don't know until too late that they're the main course."

Blaire gasped. "And you want to give these sweet little babies to him? Just so some ravenous beast can eat them? No way! We'll keep them ourselves first."

Her heart sped up as Burke leaned close.

"I hate to tell you this, but the coyotes don't care if the cats are here or at Dad's place. They'll eat them anywhere. Besides, here the cats have to contend with the ostriches too."

"But we can protect them somehow, can't we?"

The tender look in Burke's eyes made her want to lean closer and back away at the same time. "I don't know how to do that unless you put them in a cage. I've never seen a caged cat that's happy. They're meant to be out hunting and wandering around." He lifted his hat and settled it on his head again. "You don't have to decide what to do with them right away. They still have to be with their mother for a few weeks. There is one thing you can do, though."

"What's that?"

"In order for them to make good pets, they need to get used to people. You can take time every day to come out here and hold them and pet them. Once they get used to you and me, they'll be willing to let anyone hold them."

Blaire tapped her finger against her lip and frowned. "I don't know. That sounds like a tough job to me." She grinned at Burke. "But I guess if you're willing to help out, I'll make the sacrifice."

Picking up a tiny calico, Blaire cradled the kitten close. Small spots of varied colors dotted her pure white fur. "This one looks like someone sprinkled her with color. I think I'll call her Sprinkles."

The shrill ring of a phone shattered the moment. Burke glanced up toward the house.

"Isabel must be outside. She's set the phone to ring where we can hear it. Shall we see who's calling?"

"There isn't an extension out here?" Blaire glanced around.

"No, but Isabel will have put the answering machine on. We can return the call if we need to."

They put the kittens back and headed toward the house at a leisurely pace. Burke stuck his hands in his pockets. "I hate to be pushy, but this could be the guy who wants to buy those breeders. How are the books coming?"

"Uncle Ike did leave things in a mess. Plus, I know nothing about running an ostrich ranch. I've never done this type of business before. At least, not from the ground up like this. I'm making some headway, but it's slow. Can you hold off on giving the guy a price for a couple of days?"

"That shouldn't be a problem." Burke looked down at her with what appeared to be amazement. "You mean you'll have the books straightened out that fast?"

She shrugged. "That's my job. Just because this is a new

type of business doesn't make it much different than other businesses I've worked with. Mainly, I have to figure out Ike's chicken scratches in all the ledgers."

Burke laughed. "I used to tell him he should have been a doctor. He had the handwriting already figured out."

Isabel met them at the door. Her red-rimmed eyes were still wet with tears. She held a tissue to her nose.

"What's wrong?" Burke reached out to hug her. "Who called?"

"My friend Ophelia from church. Her son called." Isabel blew her nose and dabbed at her eyes. "She's been taken to the hospital. They think she's had a heart attack."

Burke pulled her into an embrace. Blaire reached over to rub Isabel's back. How had she come to care so much for this woman in such a short time? Seeing her hurting made Blaire's eyes sting with tears.

"Do you want me or Manuel to drive you to the hospital?" Burke leaned back to look at Isabel.

"No, *Mijo.*" She sniffed. "I have too much to do here. We have to get the order of blown eggs ready to go to Tucson. Besides, if I leave, who will take care of the eggs and the cooking?"

"Manuel, Blaire, and I can take care of everything."

"But there's so much to do. I don't want to burden you with more."

Blaire patted Isabel's back. "You need to be with your friend, Isabel. I can do a lot more to help out. Burke will show me the things you do that I don't know how to do. I've watched you blow out the eggs. I'm sure I can to that."

Isabel dug another tissue from her apron pocket. "I do have the eggs separated and ready. But what about the meals? I could take the time to cook something before I go."

Burke turned her around and gently pushed her in the direction of her room. "Go get ready. I'll get Manuel to drive you. Don't worry about anything. Just remember how much we'll appreciate you when you get back. I'm sure Blaire and I can handle the cooking.

Blaire watched in silence as Isabel wiped her eyes and headed to her room to get ready to leave. Did Burke have any idea what he was suggesting? Did he know her cooking skills included peanut butter sandwiches and canned soup? In Chicago she'd never worried about meals. There were great delicatessens everywhere. Here, there wasn't a fast food place for miles.

# ten

A cloud of dust rose in the air as Manuel drove down the driveway, taking his mother to the hospital to stay with Ophelia. The two women were like sisters. Isabel wanted to stay with Ophelia until her friend was discharged and could manage on her own.

Burke glanced at Blaire. Her blue eyes glistened with unshed tears. She had such a tender heart. He longed to pull her close, to cup her smooth cheek in his hand, to give her the comfort she needed. *I want to give her the love she deserves.* He shook himself mentally. Where had that come from? Sure he had an attraction to Ike's niece, but that's all it was. He clenched his jaw. *I'm not falling in love with any woman, no matter how much I admire her.* The problem was, deep down he knew it was too late. This woman had crept into his heart and made a place there. Now he would have to steel himself against the heartbreak that was sure to follow. He knew, without a doubt, that Blaire would leave one day. Facts were facts. Women weren't to be trusted.

"You probably want to get back to the books." Burke spoke more gruffly than he intended. He could see the question in Blaire's eyes and did his best to suppress the feelings of guilt that popped up. "I'll get busy on the outside chores. When Manuel gets back he'll help me."

"How long is the drive to the hospital?"

"Isabel said they took her to that new heart hospital in Tucson. That's about an hour-and-a-half drive from here. Manuel should be back in time for supper."

"Um, speaking of supper, what did you have in mind?"

"Isabel said she has some corn tortillas in the refrigerator. She put out some hamburger and suggested we make tacos. They're easy and pretty quick. I'll come in about five and help you."

Blaire looked relieved. "Thanks. I've never made tacos before. I'm pretty good at eating them, though."

"Is that a challenge?" Burke laughed. "You'd better consider carefully before you answer that one. I like tacos, but I'm nothing compared to Manuel. That boy doesn't eat tacos, he inhales them."

"Just how many tacos does he inhale?" Blaire's azure gaze took his breath away.

Burke cleared his throat and glanced down the driveway. "I've seen him eat a dozen tacos, then ask for dessert."

With her mouth opening and closing in rapid succession, Blaire looked like she was catching air. He laughed at her shocked expression. "This is just fair warning so you don't challenge him to a taco duel." He stepped off the porch. "I'll be back later."

The afternoon sped by. At 5:15 Burke managed to get to the house. He and Blaire had better get supper started before Manuel got home. As he opened the door he smelled hamburger frying. He wasn't prepared for the sight of Blaire in the kitchen. She had Isabel's apron on with the ties wrapped twice around her slender frame. She'd pulled her hair back into a ponytail, but the shorter strands curled around her face. She had her back to him, stirring the hamburger, then picking up a chunk of cheese to grate. The scene was so much like his dream of a wife and home of his own. He couldn't swallow past the lump in his throat.

"And you said you've never made tacos before." Burke grinned as Blaire jumped. Little strands of cheese now dotted the counter. One of the things he liked about her was her ability to focus on the job at hand. He didn't know which he liked more: her willingness to do the job, or the fact that he could scare her so easy.

She glared at him, then began scraping up the scattered cheese. "I know some things about tacos. What I don't know is how to make the taco shells. My mom always bought the preformed ones. The ones Isabel has are just flat."

He chuckled. "Those are corn tortillas, not taco shells. They can be used for a variety of Mexican dishes."

Burke rummaged in the cupboards until he found the skillet he wanted. With a crash of pans he pulled it free.

"No wonder Isabel doesn't let you help in the kitchen." Blaire had her hands clapped over her ears. "That sounded like you broke a cast-iron skillet."

"Nope." Burke held up the evidence. "They're too tough." He put the skillet on the stove. "I wanted this one because it's just the right size to cook a corn tortilla. You need plenty of oil, then you fry the tortilla on one side, flip it, and fold it. Let me demonstrate."

A loud buzz reverberated through the house. "That's the hatchery. I've got to go check and see what's happening. Go ahead and do the taco shells. They're pretty easy. Just don't cook them too long. Oh, and be sure to drain them good. The paper towels are over there." He pointed to the side of the sink.

Manuel pulled in the driveway as Burke left the house. The two of them headed to the hatchery and had the problem fixed before any of the eggs were in danger.

"I think I'm going to have to get some parts for the incubator soon." Burke held the door open for Manuel to enter the house. "I'll go to Globe tomorrow morning and see if they have them up there. If not, I'll have to go to Tucson the next day. I have to deliver the blown eggs anyway. I think Blaire plans to get them ready tomorrow afternoon."

Burke almost ran into Manuel's back as he stopped in the kitchen door. Peering over Manuel's shoulder, Burke could see what halted him. Blaire had her back to them and was removing what might have once been a corn tortilla from the skillet of oil. The oil-logged shell dripped grease on the stove as she swung it over to the paper towel. A long tear pulled it nearly in two. A pile of limp torn tortillas rested on the plate already.

Picking up the last of the corn tortillas, Blaire dropped it in the skillet. No sounds of popping or sizzling emanated from the frying pan. Disbelief filled him as he and Manuel moved across the kitchen. Blaire looked around. The look on her face stopped him from yelling about her ruining their supper.

"I don't think I did a very good job of making taco shells." She gestured at the plate of soggy mush.

"Why is the heat so low?"

She looked puzzled. "You said not to cook them too long. I didn't want to burn them so I turned the heat on low."

Burke resisted the urge to roll his eyes. "In order to cook them right you have to use a high heat. I should have told you that. But if you leave them in too long, they're so crispy you can't use them for taco shells."

Blaire looked like a whipped dog. "Is there any way to salvage these?"

"I think we're going to starve tonight," Manuel said. The poor boy probably thought he wouldn't live through the night without supper.

"Let's turn up the heat." Burke reached over and cranked the gas on high. "Then we'll recook the pieces of tortilla."

"But they won't make taco shells. They're all broken." Blaire lifted one with the tongs to demonstrate.

"Have you ever heard that when you have lemons you make lemonade?" Burke grinned. "Well, we'll make crisp pieces of tortilla and have taco salad instead of tacos."

Blaire and Manuel both brightened. Within fifteen minutes they were at the table eating and laughing as if taco salad had been the meal they'd planned all along.

≥∞

Blaire worked into the night on the books. She hadn't intended to stay up so late, but once again she got lost in the figures. Entering the information onto the computer was a chore, but once done, they would save an immeasurable amount of time. And retrieving the information they needed would take a matter of seconds instead of minutes or hours.

The next morning, she groaned as she dragged herself out of bed. The smell of coffee and bacon filled the house. Slipping into a blouse and a pair of shorts, she headed to the kitchen to see if Isabel had come home during the night.

"Good morning, Sleepyhead." Burke grinned at her.

She couldn't hold in the laugh. Burke stood at the stove, Isabel's apron tied loosely around him. Bacon and eggs sizzled. A plate of toast sat on the table with the plates.

"Is this your Suzy Homemaker outfit?"

Burke wiggled his eyebrows. "Just call me Sue for short. But remember, I don't do windows."

She laughed and grabbed the plates as he began to take up the eggs. "Where's Manuel?"

"Right here." Manuel walked through the door. His damp hair shone. "I checked the incubators, Burke. They're doing fine right now, but I think we need to find the parts for that one. If it goes down we'll lose several eggs."

"Sit down and eat." Burke carried the coffee to the table, then pulled out a chair for Blaire. "I'll run to Globe after breakfast and see what I can find. If they don't have the parts, I think I can rig it to work until I get to Tucson." He turned to Blaire. "Would you like to see the big city of Globe?"

She held her hand over her heart and pretended to be faint. "I'm not sure I can stand the excitement, but if you're there to protect me from those city slickers, then I'll try." She selected a piece of toast. "Is there a real estate office in Globe?"

A pained expression crossed Burke's face. His jaw tightened. "I'm sure there is. I've never needed one so I don't know where it is."

"Well, I'm getting to know the ranch well enough to list with a Realtor, I think." She tried to come up with something to ease the tension in the air. "Is Globe much bigger than Kearny?"

Manuel choked. He took a sip of coffee. "There's only a slight difference between about fifteen hundred and six or seven thousand."

Blaire blinked her eyes and tried on a dreamy expression. "Wow. Imagine that. Does this mean they have a supermarket? We could use a few groceries."

"Were you thinking of bread, peanut butter, and jelly so you can fix supper?" Burke's mouth twitched as if he were trying not to smile.

Lifting her nose in the air, Blaire gave him what she hoped was a freezing look. "I'll have you know I make the bestest peanut buster sandwiches in the whole world." She chuckled. "At least that's what my neighbor's daughter told me when I babysat for her."

"With a recommendation like that, we can't go wrong." Burke wiped his mouth, stood, and carried his dishes to the sink. "Do you think you can be ready to go in thirty minutes?"

"I'll meet you outside." Blaire watched Burke as he left. She could almost feel the hurt emanating from him. She didn't want to be the cause of that hurt, but she had to protect herself too. She knew better than to become involved with someone she worked with. She'd learned that lesson well. *Why can't we just be friends? We get along so well. I love talking, laughing, and joking with him. Lord, help me to know what's right.*

Manuel cleared his throat. His tanned face mirrored concern. "I know this is none of my business." He stopped and tore a piece off his toast. "You know, Burke is upset that you're selling the ranch."

"I know that, but I don't understand why. I'll make sure all of you are taken care of by whoever buys the place. He knows how much I want to have my own accounting firm. How can I do that here?"

Manuel chewed his toast slowly. "I only know Burke watched your uncle Ike work hard to make this place what it is today. And Ike did that for you."

Blaire stared at the young man across from her. "What do you mean?"

"Ike used to tell everyone his ranch would be yours one day. He didn't have much family, and for some reason he felt connected to you." Manuel lifted his arm, swinging it in a circle. "All this was for you."

"But he forgot to consider my wants when he did this." Blaire took her plate to the sink. "I'd better get dressed for town."

The trip to Globe was cool despite the heat of the day. Burke barely spoke. Blaire stared out at the mountains they drove over. The hills she once thought bleak and barren were covered with cacti, trees, and shrubs. She particularly liked the red stems and thick green leaves of the manzanita Burke pointed out to her. The combination of colors was almost regal.

In Globe, the only real estate agency they found was closed for the day. "I can't believe this." Blaire felt like kicking the door. "Why is it that every time I find a Realtor they're closed?"

"Maybe God's trying to tell you something." Burke shrugged when she glared at him.

She sighed. "Well, I guess I can do the grocery shopping while you find the parts you need. Just be sure to tell me what kind of jelly you like on your sandwich."

Burke grinned and escorted her back to his truck. "What if I said I like bananas best?"

"On your peanut butter? I'd say you're a little strange."

He laughed. "I think we have jelly that Isabel made. Don't worry about buying any."

Burke insisted that they shop together. He seemed relieved that she hadn't been able to connect with the Realtor. He took a tour through the town, showing her several historic landmarks and buildings. They drove to the neighboring town of Miami, passing the tall mound of dirt Burke told her was waste from the copper mines. He took her to eat at an excellent Mexican restaurant. They sat in a small, semicircular booth. Their knees almost touched. Blaire couldn't remember ever being so aware of another person. She tried her best to remember her resolve to simply be Burke's friend.

"Hey, I think I need some ice cream for the drive home." Burke swung into the left turn lane across from a Dairy Queen. "Sound good?"

"I don't know. I'm eating all this delicious and fattening Mexican food. And now you want me to add ice cream on top of that?"

"You got it."

"Sounds good." She laughed. "I'll start my diet tomorrow, right?"

They contemplated the menu side by side. Blaire couldn't think with him standing so near. When Burke suggested a dip cone, she agreed. She had no idea what other selections were offered.

"Here, I'll carry this to the truck for you." Burke lifted the two cones.

"I can carry my own." Blaire stretched out her hand.

Burke raised his eyebrows. "You? I haven't seen you stumble and fall lately. I figure it's like an earthquake. You're due to slip any moment." He gave her a mocking grin. "I'll carry the cones."

Blaire made a face at him and opened the door. Burke was still grinning at her. He didn't see the family headed in their direction. An eager young girl plowed into him as he stepped through the door. Burke stumbled. One cone flew up and landed on Blaire's shoulder. He grabbed the girl to keep her from falling. The second cone smashed into his chest.

"Well, we're a matched set. I think you stood too close to the fault line, Mr. Earthquake." Blaire plucked the cone from her shoulder and used the napkins she'd picked up to attempt to wipe the ice cream off her blouse.

Burke took one look at her, his chuckle rumbling deep in his chest as he scooped melting ice cream off his shirt.

# eleven

Blaire heard a vehicle coming down the driveway as she stepped out of the shower. "Oh, please be Isabel. I don't want to have to try to cook again." She wrapped a small towel around her head and tugged on shorts and a T-shirt that featured a picture of a cute kitten circled by the words "Purrrrfectly Loveable."

As she ran a brush through her hair, a loud knock echoed through the house. She frowned. Isabel wouldn't knock. Burke would have used the kitchen door, and he wouldn't knock, either. Besides, like her, he was trying to wash off the remains of today's ice-cream bath.

She finished her hair and headed to the door. The banging began again, this time sounding as if the door would fall apart. "I'm coming." She trotted barefoot across the living room.

Through the glass she could see a giant bunch of roses atop two legs. The right foot lifted and headed for the door. She jerked it open before the foot connected.

"May I help you?"

"I'm looking for Blaire Mackenzie."

The high feminine voice startled Blaire. She'd assumed the jeans-clad legs belonged to a man.

"I'm Blaire."

The roses moved, and Blaire could see dark brown eyes peering at her through the flowers. The eyes appeared to be framed by hair dyed a vivid shade of royal blue.

"These are for you."

The huge bouquet moved in Blaire's direction. She groped

through the foliage to grasp the large vase beneath the greenery.

"Flowers for me?" Blaire managed to find a handhold on the vase. "Thank you."

"No problem. Hope you enjoy them." The slender girl sauntered down the walkway to a blue minivan whose color clashed with her royal blue hair.

Blaire backed through the doorway, turning the flowers sideways. They still brushed the door frame, the fragrant blossoms swinging toward her as they cleared the opening. The clump of booted feet crossing the kitchen told her she wasn't alone anymore.

"What's this? Need some help?" She shivered as Burke's hands brushed across hers. He lifted the bouquet and took them to the coffee table. "You want them here?"

"I guess." Blaire swung the door closed and followed him. "I wonder who they're from."

"My guess is someone who has plenty of money." Burke straightened, tilted his hat back, and scratched his head. "There must be at least two dozen roses there, maybe more."

Blaire leaned over and inhaled the fragrance. She loved roses. "They're beautiful." She glanced at Burke from the corner of her eye. Had he sent them? Could he have gotten the wrong impression from her? "I can't imagine who could have sent them."

Burke rubbed his jaw. His eyes twinkled. "I don't suppose you want to open the card." He lifted the small florist card with one finger, then let it drop again.

"I didn't see that." Blaire snatched the envelope and pulled out the card. She resisted the urge to turn her back on Burke. Glancing down, she gasped. She felt as if someone had kicked her. The card fluttered to the floor.

"You okay? You're white as a sheet." Burke took hold of her arm.

"I'm fine." She stared at the white square on the carpet. "How could he?"

"How could he what?" Burke's hold tightened on her arm. "I think you need to sit down."

Blaire sank down on the couch. Her whole body trembled. She didn't know if the shaking was from anger, shock, or what. Her mind refused to grasp the words on the card.

"May I?" Burke reached for the note. She shrugged, unable to look at him. " 'Please forgive me. I love you. Richard.' "

Silence filled the room. "Isn't this the cad who dumped you?"

She nodded. Blaire reached for the vase. Her hands shook. She pulled them back, placing them between her legs.

"Would you like me to get rid of these for you?"

"Do you think the trash can is big enough?" She cleared her throat. Her attempt at levity fell flat. Blaire pressed her fingertips into the corners of her eyes. She wanted to scream and kick, but she didn't want Burke to see how badly she hurt.

"Manuel told me that Isabel called. Her friend Ophelia just got home from the hospital. Isabel is staying with her for a day or two. I could take the flowers over there for Ophelia. She and Isabel don't have to know where they came from."

The fragrance of roses, which Blaire normally loved, was causing her head to pound. She forced a smile that probably looked more like a grimace. "Kind of like giving flowers from a funeral to the residents of nursing homes, right?" She turned away from Burke. Right now she couldn't take the look of concern on his face. "That's a good idea. I'm sure Ophelia will love the flowers."

"I'll take them right away." Burke rested his hand lightly on her shoulder. "Will you be okay?"

She wanted to scream, "No, I'll never be okay again. My insides are ripped apart." Instead, she choked back a sob and nodded.

❧

Burke set the vase of flowers on the floor of the truck as far from the driver's side as possible. He opened the vent and cracked his window, hoping the cloying smell would be drawn out. He wanted to throw the flowers, vase and all, as far as he could, but he had already committed to giving them to Ophelia.

He didn't take long delivering the flowers. Ophelia, worn out from the trip home from the hospital, wasn't up to company. Burke left so Isabel could give her full attention to her friend. They both loved the flowers.

Within an hour Burke was bumping along a dirt track near the Gila River. Twisted mesquite trees draped shade near the water. He parked his truck and walked over to sit on the bank. A dribble of dirt cascaded down the embankment.

Burke's hand curled around a clump of grass, pulling it up by the roots. He tossed the missile into the midst of the flowing water. The heavy dirt on the roots made a splash. Ripples started to spread, then blended with the movement of the stream. He thought if he had Richard here he would throw him into the middle of the river. He'd never felt so protective and vulnerable as he had when he'd seen the wounded look on Blaire's face today.

He hadn't attended church with Isabel or Blaire since the Sunday when the pastor talked about green pastures, but he hadn't been able to get the message out of his mind, either. "God, I don't understand this. I don't understand You. Why is this happening to Blaire? If this is Your green pasture like the pastor said, then why does she want to leave, and why is she being hurt? I don't know if I even believe that Scripture is right."

Burke plucked another clump of grass from the bank and hurled it into the water. This was his place to come for quiet. He liked to sit and think. Sometimes, he'd talked to God, but he hadn't done that in a long time. After his grandmother had died, this place had been a refuge for him. He'd never even brought a friend with him.

He picked a weed and began to pull the leaves from the stem. "Take the first part of that Psalm. The part that says You're my shepherd and I won't want. Well, that's not true. I remember praying with Mom when I was young. I asked you to be my Savior. But I still had wants. I wanted a mother to be there and raise me. I wanted a grandmother who didn't desert me. I wanted someone who really cared, and I don't think You ever did."

Burke wasn't sure how this conversation had changed from Blaire to himself. Tears burned in his eyes. A lump built in his throat. "Isn't the Bible saying You'll take care of our wants? Well, You never did that for me, God, and now it seems like You're not doing that for Blaire, either."

He put his hat on the ground beside him and covered his face with his hands. Pressing his thumbs into his eyes, he tried to stem his emotions. "I'm so confused, Lord. I don't want to love any woman. I know they can't be trusted. But I can't seem to help myself with Blaire. She's like the half of me that's been missing all along." He scrubbed at his face.

"Help me, Lord. I don't know why I feel so protective of Blaire. We've only known each other a few weeks, yet I feel as if I've known her forever. I think about her all the time. I want to run from her, but I can't." The water rippled and swirled below his feet.

Unwanted memories of Julie swam before him. His high school sweetheart. Beautiful, vivacious Julie, every guy's dream, but she'd belonged to him. They were engaged when he left for college. Only one more year and she would graduate. They'd planned to marry when he came home for the summer. "Lord, help me to know Blaire won't be like Julie. Help me know what to do."

No answers came. Burke didn't feel any peace. He wasn't even sure God had heard him or cared. The breeze dried the excess moisture from his eyes, and after awhile he picked up his hat, climbed into the truck, and drove away feeling as confused as ever.

The ranch was quiet when he returned. Late afternoon shadows covered the house. He opened the front door and stuck his head in. "Hello?" The house echoed with an empty silence. Where had Blaire gone?

In the small house he shared with Manuel, Burke found a note saying he had gone to town to see some of his friends. Manuel had done most of the evening chores and had listed what was left to do.

Burke stalked to the barn. This still didn't explain where Blaire could be. Her car was parked out front so she had to be within walking distance. She wouldn't have gone with Manuel. *Why am I so worried about her? I don't want to watch out for her. I'd like it better if she just sold the ranch and left.* Deep down, Burke knew he was lying to himself. He couldn't stand the thought of her leaving.

Stopping inside the barn door, Burke waited for his eyes to adjust to the darkness. The late afternoon sun didn't light the interior. A sound near the back of the barn caught his attention. He smiled. The kittens. He'd forgotten about them.

Stepping carefully, he crept past the various implements cluttering the floor. His breath caught in his throat. Blaire was stretched out on her back in a pile of hay, her hair fanning out like a cloud around her head. The four kittens toddled across her stomach, trying to jump on one another. Each vied for her attention, their little tails stick-straight in the air. Blaire giggled as one tumbled down onto her neck.

Burke had never seen such an arresting sight. He leaned against a wall and watched them play. Blaire rolled over onto her side. As if suddenly aware of his presence, she looked up.

"Oh." She jumped up, kittens rolling off into the hay. She scooped them up. "I'm sorry." She held the little furballs next to her cheek, then flushed. "I didn't hear you come home." She pulled some pieces of hay from her hair and tried to brush off her shorts and top.

"I just got home." Burke crossed his arms over his chest, fighting the urge to wrap his arms around this alluring woman. "I stopped in to see my dad. He asked if we'd like to join him for supper."

Blaire's eyes narrowed. "What, and miss my famous peanut butter and jelly? I believe I'm offended." She stuck her nose in the air. The calico kitten pulled herself up on Blaire's shirt and nuzzled her neck. She giggled and tucked in her chin. "Sprinkles, stop that. I'm trying to be serious here."

"I didn't realize you'd gotten them so tamed." Burke walked over and picked up one of the kittens still on the ground. "You must have been spending a lot of time with them."

"I've never had a baby animal like this. I didn't realize they could be so cuddly." Blaire lifted the kitten up to her face. A tiny paw batted her nose.

"This is probably their cutest age." Burke squatted down and waved a piece of straw in front of the kittens. One pounced, then another. In a moment they were falling all over each other to catch the straw that kept eluding them. "I think they're ready to give away. Would you like to take them over to the ranch this evening?"

Blaire sank down into the hay. "I worry that they'll just end up being eaten by the coyotes. They're so little." She rubbed a kitten against her cheek.

"We can put them in my dad's barn. There's lots of hay there where they can hide. They'll be well fed. These kittens won't be in any more danger there than they're in here."

The kitten in Blaire's arms jumped to the ground, landing on one of the other kittens. They rolled over in a mock battle.

She smiled, her azure eyes seeking out his. "I don't think they're in any danger here."

Standing up, she stretched. "Do we have chores to do before we leave for your dad's ranch? I'm already getting hungry."

Burke grabbed a can of feed and followed her out of the barn. He grabbed her arm. She stopped and looked at him.

"I don't understand." Burke stared into her peaceful eyes. No sign of hurt remained. "When I left, you were so upset. Now you act as if nothing has happened. Why?"

A smile washed over her. "I had a talk with Jesus. He heals wounds." She sauntered over to the ostrich pen where Burke was taking the food and leaned against a small tree outside the fence. Burke stopped beside her. The ostriches stalked across the enclosure toward them.

"When Richard left me, I thought my world would end. I blamed God at first. But the more I hurt, the more I realized my need to give my whole life to Jesus. I had prayed for Jesus to come into my heart as a child, but I'd never committed my life to Him as an adult. I was still running the show."

Blaire picked a leaf from the tree and twisted it in her fingers. "I can't explain the change when I put Jesus in charge of everything. In fact, I've been struggling with this issue still."

"How's that?"

"Well, I tend to think I know what God wants for me and then run with it. I forget that because I don't see the whole plan, there may be changes I don't know about."

Burke shook his head. "I don't think I understand."

Taking a deep breath, Blaire pursed her lips and let the air out slowly. "It's like the ranch. When I first heard about my inheritance, I was sure this was what God wanted for me. Then when I saw the ranch, I knew this couldn't be God's plan. Now, I'm not sure what to think. The more I'm here, the more I want to stay. This place has been a balm for me. I've never felt such peace." She brushed the hair back from her face. "On the other hand, I still feel I'm a city girl. I don't belong in a place like this."

Something grabbed Burke's pant leg and tugged. He looked down. One of the kittens was halfway up his shin, digging its tiny claws in to climb farther. "Hey, fella." He reached down and plucked the kitten off his leg. "Look who followed us out here." He held out the kitten to Blaire.

"You bad kitty." She took the baby from him and snuggled it to her face. "I'll put him back in the barn, while you feed the ostriches."

Burke started to head for the feed dishes when he noticed the ostriches acting funny. They circled a small pile of rocks about ten feet into the pen.

"Blaire, I think we've got trouble."

She turned. An ostrich neck snaked out toward the rocks. "Hssst!" A kitten jumped back from the ostrich. The fur spiked straight out from the kitten's back. A noise of half yowl, half growl, drifted through the fence.

Blaire grabbed his arm. "It's Sprinkles. You've got to save her."

# twelve

"I don't know how I can help her." Burke started to circle to the gate. Maybe he could distract the ostriches long enough for the kitten to get to the fence. He heard another series of hisses as one of the ostriches tried to peck at the kitten. The poor kitten's tail looked like a pine tree with the branches perpendicular to the trunk.

"What are you doing?" Blaire hurried after him, clutching the other kitten.

He stopped with his hand on the gate, lifted his hat, then set it back on his head. "I want you to go to the part of the fence closest to the kitten. When you see the ostriches come my way, call her to you."

"But you could get hurt."

Burke gazed into Blaire's eyes and saw fear. Did she care about him? Was this concern different from the feelings she would have for someone else in this situation? Somehow, he wanted to hope this was special.

"I'll be fine. These ostriches know me. Besides, I'm good at rescuing damsels in distress, right?" He slipped the catch off the gate and let himself through. He waited until Blaire returned to the area closest to the kitten.

Gliding toward the feeding pans, Burke shook the can of feed in his hand. Usually, he slipped the feed in while on the other side of the fence. This time he hoped he could use the feed to distract the ostriches without angering the male. He shook the can a little harder. The feed rattled. The ostriches looked around.

The male ostrich lifted his head. He swung around. The

females headed for the feeder. The male focused on Burke. He stalked across the pen like an avenging protector. Burke's heart pounded. He backed toward the fence. Maybe this wasn't the best idea.

Glancing to the side, he saw Blaire beckoning to the kitten. She called softly, but the male ostrich hesitated. He tilted his head and turned to look back at the rocks. Burke rattled the can.

In a flash of movement, the ostrich charged Burke. His wings stood out to the side. His neck stretched out, and his feet dug into the dirt. Breathing hard, Burke reached behind him. He felt the gate catch. He jerked the gate open and tumbled through, slamming the gate shut just before the enraged male reached him.

৯

Blaire paused in her attempts to get the terrified kitten to come to her. She couldn't believe how fast the male ostrich was running at Burke. She opened her mouth to scream, but there wasn't time. Burke nearly fell through the gate. The feed can dropped to the ground, spilling pellets in the dust.

"Mew."

She looked back to see the kitten slinking toward the fence and her. The ostrich must have heard the noise. He didn't slow as the gate slammed, instead circling around and racing across the pen. The terrified kitten flattened herself against the ground. She hissed. Her fur stood on end. The ostrich extended his neck, beak wide open.

"No!" Blaire waved her hand at him, trying to stop the charge. She wished for something to throw, but there was no time. The male grabbed the calico's tail. Raising his long neck, he flipped the kitten into the air. Yowling, the tiny cat flipped end over end through the air. Blaire held her breath. She'd never felt so helpless in all her life. Sprinkles flew over the fence and landed in the dirt with a thud.

Burke passed her as they both headed toward the small, inert form. He knelt down and touched the body. The kitten leaped up. On tiptoes she hissed and spit. Blaire covered her mouth, trying to hold in the laughter. Sprinkles looked like a caricature of a cat with its tail in an electrical outlet.

"Whoa there, Sweetheart. I just want to see if you're okay." Burke held out his hand and continued to speak soft and low. Within minutes, the kitten had clambered into his lap, purring loudly enough to wake the neighbors if they had any.

"The knight in shining armor wins again." Blaire chuckled.

Burke grinned. "That wasn't exactly how I planned to get said damsel out of the pen. At least she's forgiven me."

"Well, I see you're right about the kittens. Now that they're weaned, we should take them to the ranch this evening. Somehow I can't picture cows running around with kittens dangling from their mouths." Even though Blaire knew the decision was right, she still would miss the kittens when they were gone.

❧

June arrived. Blaire couldn't believe the heat in Arizona. She didn't remember the Midwest ever being this hot, even with the humidity factor. She had the books straightened out and all the ranch's business on the computer. Several of the breeders and young ostriches had been sold. She knew she had decisions to make that she'd been putting off. Did she want to sell the ranch or did she want to stay? She prayed every day for an answer, but nothing came. She knew she would probably be happier in the city. Hadn't she always loved her life there?

However, country life had grown on her. The majesty of the mountains around her home never failed to amaze her. The gorgeous sunrises and sunsets made her catch her breath in wonder. Most of all, the peace and time of refreshment with Jesus had been such a healing balm that she didn't want to leave. She'd even begun to enjoy all the attention she received at church.

Only two issues marred the horizon. Richard had continued to bother her. He sent her E-mails and had called several times. She never returned the calls or the E-mails, thinking he would take the hint. Since she hadn't heard from him in two weeks, she assumed her strategy had worked.

The other issue was Burke. Somehow, she'd fallen in love with him. She hadn't wanted to. She tried to stay away from him. She knew how dangerous it was to fall for someone she worked with. Despite all her protections against him, Burke had wormed his way into her heart. She didn't know what to do about him.

♥

"I need to talk to all of you." Blaire sat at the table with Isabel, Manuel, and Burke. They all looked at her. An expectant hush filled the air.

"What is it, *Mija?*" Isabel stood and began to clear the supper dishes.

"No, Isabel, sit down." Blaire touched her friend's arm. "I want you to hear what I have to say."

Taking a deep breath, Blaire released a silent prayer for help. "I've enjoyed getting to know you. I can see why Uncle Ike loved you so much."

Burke's eyes narrowed. Manuel ran his finger over his unused spoon. Isabel folded her hands and lowered them to her lap.

"I can't decide what God wants me to do. I've prayed and have no clear answers. I've finished the books and know the value of the ranch." She wanted to close her eyes but didn't dare. "I know Burke is taking a delivery of blown eggs to Tucson tomorrow. I'm planning to ride along and visit a couple of real estate agents. I've already been in touch with them."

Burke's hands slapped down on the table. He pushed himself up.

"Wait." Blaire covered his hand with hers. She met his

eyes, pleading silently with him. "Please, hear me out."

Burke sank back down. His fingers continued gripping the table.

"I know this is your life. I want to make sure you are taken care of, especially Isabel. If I do find a buyer, I'll see if they are compatible and will continue to keep you on here. If they don't want you to stay, then I will provide enough from the sale to get Isabel set up with a place of her own." She looked at Isabel. Misery gripped her heart as she saw the tears in the older woman's eyes.

*"Mija,* that is a wonderful gesture. You don't have to do this."

"I know, but I care so much for you, Isabel. You were all special to my uncle, and you've become special to me. I don't want to leave you without a job or a means of support."

"Whatever you do will be fine, *Mija."* Isabel patted Blaire's cheek and began to clear the table.

"Sounds good to me." Manuel tossed the spoon back on the table. "I'm heading for town."

Blaire focused on her hands. She didn't want to look at Burke. Would he be able to understand? He wanted so much for her to keep the ranch, but she wasn't sure she could stay around him much longer.

A large callused hand brushed her cheek. She looked up. Burke leaned close. "Thank you. It means so much that you're thinking of Isabel." He stood and headed out the door without another word. Blaire escaped to her room before the lump in her throat turned into a bout of tears.

❧

The day in Tucson flew past. Blaire loved visiting the woman who bought the eggs from them. She showed them her workshop. Decorated eggs lined the shelves on the walls. She showed them a lamp whose base was made from a hollow ostrich egg with a scene etched on it. When Blaire praised the artistry, the woman brought out some more lamps for her to look at. Blaire couldn't decide if she liked the one with the giraffes or the one picturing the resurrection best.

In the afternoon, Blaire and Burke visited the Realtors. Blaire decided which agent she wanted to work with and listed the ranch for three months to see what would happen. She thought if God wanted her to sell the ranch, He would provide a buyer in that short period. The Realtor, Janice Burns, was horrified. "You can't expect to sell such a large property in such a short time period. It just doesn't happen." Blaire had been adamant. Janice finally conceded and wrote up the contract.

By the time they left the real estate office, dark clouds were building in the distance. "Looks like we might get some rain today." Burke lifted his face to the wind. "I wonder if the monsoons are coming early."

"The air feels a little muggy." Blaire tugged at the collar of her blouse. "At least it's a little cooler."

Burke grinned at her, his eyes twinkling. "What do you say we do something special before we have supper and head home?"

"What did you have in mind?" Blaire couldn't help being suspicious. He was grinning like a Cheshire cat.

"Let's go to the zoo. We're not far from there." He looked like a little boy pleading with his mom. He leaned close as if whispering a secret in her ear. "They have giraffes."

"Why didn't you say so?" Blaire started walking to the truck. She laughed at the astonished look on his face. "You didn't expect me to give in this easily, did you? Now you know what happens when you say the magic word—giraffe."

It proved to be the perfect time to visit the zoo. Due to the clouds rolling in and the cooler temperature, many of the animals that normally slept through the hot afternoons were awake. Blaire decided that going to the zoo with Burke was better than having a young child along. From the moment they crossed through the gate onto the zoo grounds, he changed from a grown man to a little boy. He led Blaire from one exhibit to another. They watched the lions, the tigers, and the bears. He grabbed her hand and had her almost running when they heard the polar bears were swimming. First, they stood above, watching the huge bears cavort in the water with a bowling ball, acting as if it weighed no more than a beach ball. Then Burke led her underground to the windows looking out into the water. Bears turned somersaults and swam effortlessly in the deep water.

"They're so graceful."

Burke could hear the awe in Blaire's voice. She stood close, her shoulder brushing against his. He wanted to put his arm around her and pull her tight against him. What would it feel like to stand here with her head resting against his shoulder? He knew he had to be careful. She was his boss, and he didn't want to cross a line that would make her run.

"I think I hear the giraffes calling."

She turned and made a face at him. "Giraffes don't call. Besides, what would they say?"

He put his hand on her back, guiding her to the exhibit. A mother pushed a stroller down the ramp, and he moved closer to Blaire. "Be quiet. Let me listen." He tilted his head to the side. Blaire's mouth twitched as she watched him. "Ah, yes. They're saying something about seeing a beautiful young woman who has great taste in collectibles."

Burke held his breath. Had he gone too far? Would Blaire be offended with his flirting? He hadn't meant to; the words had slipped out.

Blaire's laugh set him at ease. She gazed across the fence at the stately giraffes. "I don't know why Uncle Ike didn't start a giraffe ranch. I would've loved raising them."

"But you would have a hard time eating them."

Blaire looked horrified. "I won't eat ostrich, either."

"Oops! Too late. I believe Isabel uses a lot of ground ostrich in her recipes." He leaned forward, studying Blaire's face. "Are you turning green?"

Thunder rumbled in the distance, cutting off Blaire's reply.

"We'd better finish up the zoo." Burke gestured at the sky. "Looks like if we don't get through soon, we'll get wet."

They stopped briefly to watch the monkeys chase one another through the tree limbs in their cage. The sky darkened, lightning flashed, and thunder rumbled louder and closer. Burke took her hand and led her through the maze of paths that wound past the various animals.

As they walked past the last row of cages housing the assorted members of the ape family, large drops of water began to splat on the sidewalk. Burke could see a deluge heading their way. Spotting a tarp set up over a nearby lawn, he pulled Blaire in that direction. They didn't have time to reach their car or even the covered eating area. Several other zoo visitors joined them in their temporary shelter.

"We'll wait here. The rain shouldn't last long," Burke said.

The skies opened and rain poured down. The air cooled. Burke pulled Blaire closer to the edge to allow two more people under the tarp. Lightning flashed, followed by a crack of thunder that shook the ground.

Blaire looked up at him and grinned. She said something. He shook his head, trying to tell her he hadn't heard. She turned and leaned close. Burke tried to concentrate on her words and not her closeness.

"How long will this last?"

Burke leaned close, his mouth beside her ear so she could hear. "It should let up in a few minutes. These downpours don't last too long."

An ear-splitting crack of thunder drowned Blaire's reply. Burke gestured for her to repeat what she'd said.

"And you call this a rain?" Everyone heard Blaire's words during a short lull in the storm. "In Chicago we get rain like this, and it lasts all day." Blaire's eyes sparkled with mirth. The wind picked up, blowing her hair across her face. She brushed the strands away from her eyes and stepped away from him.

Burke reached out to bring her back from the edge of the tarp, but he was too late. A sudden gust of wind lifted the center of the covering. Rainwater that had collected in a pocket cascaded down in a waterfall. Blaire's eyes widened. Water gushed over her face and down her back. Her mouth formed a perfect O. She looked as if someone had dumped a bucket of water on her head.

Burke couldn't resist. Biting back a laugh, he gestured at the storm. "Never mess with an Arizona monsoon."

# thirteen

Blaire's hair and clothes were almost dry by the time they pulled up in front of the house. "Oh, I can't wait to get a shower." She held up her hand to stop Burke before he spoke. "I know I've already had one shower." She wrinkled her nose at him. "I was referring to a real washing with soap and shampoo."

"Was I going to say something?" Burke feigned an innocent expression. He chuckled. "Come on. I'll help carry in the groceries. I think we can get them all in one trip."

The night breeze carried the aroma of rain-washed ground. Crickets and cicadas sang their nightly chorus. Blaire tilted her head back to look at the sky. Remnants of clouds drifted across a star-sprinkled sky. A nearly full moon bathed the earth in a golden glow. She couldn't remember seeing anything this beautiful in the city. There, the tall buildings and bright lights blocked any view of the sky.

"You gonna stand out here all night? That ice cream you're carrying may not adjust to the heat."

Blaire hurried to where Burke held the door open for her. "Sorry. I just can't get over how much sky there is out here."

"If you want, we can sit in the swing for awhile after we put away the groceries. This is the best time of year to sit outside."

Blaire looked up at Burke as she passed him. His hat and the darkness shadowed his eyes. Was this an innocent request? Could she sit beside him and ignore the attraction she had for him? Somehow it didn't seem to matter so much right now. They'd had such a wonderful day, she didn't want their time together to end.

"I think I'd like that." She smiled and headed for the kitchen.

Opening the freezer without turning on the light, Blaire began putting ice cream containers away. Burke flipped on the light as he entered the kitchen behind her.

"Hmm. This looks good."

Blaire shut the freezer and turned to see what he was talking about. "Are you thinking of eating again? What did Isabel leave out for you?"

She walked over to the table and peered around Burke. There on the table stood a large basket filled with greenery. Shooting up from the fake green plants were a dozen heart-shaped cookies. Decorated in various pastel shades, each cookie said "I love you" in sparkling gold icing. A multi-hued pastel ribbon wound around the gold basket holding the arrangement. A small gold card nestled in the bottom of the basket. Blaire's name was inscribed on the card.

"Somehow I don't think Isabel made this." Burke fingered the colorful ribbon. "She's not usually this fancy."

A sense of dread descended on Blaire as she reached for the envelope. She slipped the card out.

"I can't believe he's doing this. I don't understand." Tears welled up in her eyes. "Listen to this." She couldn't keep the anger out of her voice. "My dearest Blaire. I can't get you off my mind. I'm coming to see you tomorrow. I love you more than ever. Your loving fiancé, Richard."

She threw the card at the basket of cookies. "How dare he consider himself to still be engaged to me? Who does he think he is? Here he takes off with the secretary, breaks our engagement, puts everyone out of a job, and he thinks I should forget all that."

Burke wrapped his arms around her, pulling her close.

"I'm ranting, aren't I?" Blaire could barely speak past the lump in her throat.

"You have every right to rant." The comforting rumble of Burke's voice made her relax against his chest. His hand rubbed her back. Tears slid down her cheeks.

"I'm so angry I could spit."

Burke hugged her closer. "Please save the spitting for tomorrow."

She slapped her hand against his chest. "Don't you make me laugh when I'm doing my best to throw a fit." A picture of her spitting on Richard in the expensive suit that he always wore flashed across her mind. Something between a sob and a giggle escaped her.

"You aren't laughing, are you?"

She tipped her head back. His green eyes caught and held hers. His mouth quirked up in a smile. Blaire pushed away from him. She wanted him to hold her too much. The temptation was too great. "Thanks for listening. I think I'm going to pass on the swing tonight. I need some time alone."

Burke gazed down at her. She couldn't look away. He reached up and cupped her cheek. She wanted to close her eyes and lean into the caress, but she couldn't. He nodded and stepped back.

"I'll see you in the morning." When he turned and left the kitchen, she felt as if some part of her was missing.

☙

Early the next afternoon, a rented sports car pulled up in the drive. Blaire watched from the bedroom window as Richard climbed out from behind the wheel. He paused before closing the door, obviously surveying the ranch. With a flip of his wrist, he swung the door shut and sauntered toward the house.

"Thank You, Jesus. I can't believe the peace You've given me." Blaire hadn't been able to sleep the night before after Burke left. Instead, she'd spent a couple hours praying and studying her Bible. She'd come to realize that worrying about Richard wasn't what God wanted. She turned the matter over to God and spent the rest of the night sleeping peacefully. Now, she felt nothing. No anger, remorse, attraction. There seemed to be a shield between her and the world, as if God was protecting her.

"Blaire, you have a visitor." Isabel stood at the doorway, a look of concern on her face.

"Thank you, Isabel. I'll be right there." Blaire gave a final glance in the mirror before following Isabel to the living room. Richard stood with his back to her, his hands clasped together behind his back in what he always referred to as his board-of-director's stance. As he turned, she could see the frown on his face.

Richard caught sight of her, and his handsome features melted into the smile that won every heart at Bennett and Sons. He stretched out his hands. "Blaire, I've missed you so much." He waited, and she knew he expected her to come to him.

"How's Vanessa, Richard?"

The perfect smile showing his perfect teeth faltered. "Oh, that." He gave a slight laugh. "Surely you don't hold a little indiscretion against me, Sweetheart. Every bridegroom gets a touch of cold feet and wants one last fling."

"I don't know any who have done that other than you, and I am not your sweetheart." An image of her spitting at Richard crossed her mind. She bit her lip to keep from smiling. Somehow that vision looked more and more tempting.

Richard managed to look wounded. "We're engaged, Blaire. I have the right to call my future wife by an endearment if I want, don't I?"

"In case you've forgotten, you broke our engagement, Richard. I have no idea why you're here, and I'd like for you to leave."

Striding across the room, Richard came within what she was sure would be spitting distance before he stopped. "Why, I came to see you and your new holdings. I know the wedding has to be delayed, but I'm sure we can arrange the ceremony by the end of summer."

Blaire's hands closed into fists. "Richard, understand this. I am not now, nor am I ever going to marry you. Our engagement was a major mistake on my part."

"Ah, Blaire." He reached out to touch her, and she backed up a step. "Always independent, weren't you? Come, let's go outside, and you can show me your inheritance."

She stared at him. "Is that what this is all about, Richard? Are you suddenly interested in me again because I've inherited Uncle Ike's ranch?"

"Of course not." The million-dollar grin spread over his face again. "I did read up on ostriches, though. They are fascinating creatures, aren't they? What kind of ostriches do you have here?"

"The kind with long necks and long legs." Blaire headed out the door, hoping she could walk him to his car and hasten his departure.

Richard chuckled. "No, Dear. I found out that some ostriches are much more valuable than others. I wondered what type you have."

"We have South African blacks." She reached the sports car and turned. Richard was halfway to the first ostrich pens. *I'm gonna start spitting any minute, and he won't like it.* She stalked across the yard after him. From the corner of her eye, she saw Isabel walking toward the house with Burke and Manuel. She must have gone to tell them that Richard had arrived. Maybe they could all take turns spitting on him. *Lord, I have got to get my thoughts under control. Please help me not to be bitter over the way Richard treated me.*

Richard stood outside a pen of juvenile males, studying the ostriches, rubbing his chin. She remembered the gesture from all the times he would lean back in his chair in the office as if in deep thought about a client's accounts.

"So, Richard, have you reopened Bennett and Sons, or are all those people still out of work?"

His eyes widened in a totally innocent expression. "Why, Blaire, that was only a temporary layoff. All the workers who wanted to return are back to work."

"How many?" Blaire leaned forward, wondering if she would get a straight answer.

"Well, several of our former employees had already gotten other jobs by the time the layoff was over. Consequently, we didn't hire them back."

"How many are working now?"

He cleared his throat and turned back to the ostriches.

"What did you say, Richard? I don't think I heard you."

"Four." His composure slipped as he snapped at her. "We have four employees working right now."

She nodded, thinking of all her coworkers who'd been devastated last December when their place of employment had closed down. She hoped Richard was stating the truth when he said they had jobs. She studied his profile. What on earth had she ever seen in this pompous buffoon? Had she been so blinded by money, looks, and prestige that she'd overlooked his egotism? The thought was embarrassing.

"Richard, there is nothing here for you. If you came hoping to woo me into marrying you so you could have access to my money, it won't work. Now please leave."

Before she could step back, Richard's arm swept around her, hauling her close to him. "I always liked your feistiness, Blaire." He leaned close, his dark blue eyes holding none of the smile on his face. "I know you're just a little angry and hurt, but you'll come around. Now, why don't you show me this ranch I'm going to help you with when we're married?"

"I believe Miss Mackenzie asked you to leave."

Richard loosened his grip, and Blaire stumbled back. Burke caught her and pulled her to his side.

"Is this the hired help?" Richard gave Burke a condescending look.

"This is Burke Dunham, my ranch manager." Blaire turned to Isabel and Manuel, standing slightly behind Burke. "This is Isabel Ortega and her son, Manuel. They work here too."

Richard clasped his hands behind his back and rocked on his heels. "I've heard that in border states like this, one can hire illegal aliens for much less pay. That's practicing good business, Blaire."

Anger raced through her. Isabel grabbed Manuel's arm. Burke stiffened beside her.

"Isabel and Manuel are U.S. citizens, Richard. I don't appreciate your insinuations. They are valuable to the running of this ranch."

"Would you like to leave on your own, or would you like for Manuel and me to escort you to your car?" Burke's jaw clenched as he finished speaking.

Blaire smiled at him, hoping to ease some of the tension. Burke glanced down at her, then placed a hand on her shoulder as if trying to reassure her everything would be all right.

"Oh, I see what's happening here." The sneer on Richard's face didn't add to his good looks. "You want me to leave because you've already replaced me. Is that your game, Blaire? Exactly what does this country bumpkin have?"

"I haven't replaced you with anyone, Richard. I didn't come out here looking for a man to marry. Burke is my manager and a friend. I couldn't run this ranch without him."

"So, you think I can't work with these stupid birds?" Richard's face reddened. "I'm telling you, I read up on them before I came out here. Watch this." He whirled around, opened the gate, and strode into the pen before they could stop him.

The young ostriches lifted their heads. They tilted them to one side. Richard continued to move toward them, although his stride had shortened.

"Richard, come out of there before you get hurt."

"I will not get hurt. I read that only the males who are mating are dangerous."

The dark-feathered ostriches spread out, circling and moving closer to the strange human. Blaire turned to Burke. He had his arms folded across his chest. He flashed a grin back at Manuel. They didn't say anything.

Suddenly, the ostriches began pulling at Richard's coat. Blaire remembered the ostriches doing the same thing with her skirt. Richard tried to back away, but more birds were behind him. He lost his balance and fell to one knee. The birds poked at him with their beaks. He fell on his face, covering his head with his arms. With expressions of glee, the youngsters entered into their new game. They began rolling Richard around the pen, pulling at him. Blaire heard a tear and saw a button pop off. She hated to think how much his suit cost. It wouldn't be worth anything now.

Richard yelled. The ostriches tilted their heads and stopped. Richard lunged upward, pivoting from left to right as if searching for the gate. He spotted Blaire and started to stumble toward her. The ostriches knocked him down.

"Will they hurt him?" She felt more than heard Burke chuckling behind her.

"Oh, I imagine he'll be a little sore, but they're just playing."

An ostrich plucked at a sleeve. It tore free. A foot stepped on a pant leg. Richard rolled closer to the gate, and the pant's leg tore. Within moments, Richard's fancy clothes were in tatters. He stumbled up and grabbed the catch. He swung the gate open and fell through. His jacket remained a pull toy in the pen. His shirt, minus the sleeves, only covered his shoulders. His pants, partially intact, were torn shorter than any shorts Blaire had ever seen. Only his tie remained unscathed, a ludicrous reminder of his once-perfect attire. Blaire looked away, trying hard to feel some sympathy.

Burke stepped forward and closed the pen before the ostriches escaped. Richard staggered to his feet. He tried to pull the ribbons of his pants together, but to no avail. With a look of pure hatred at the group watching him, he headed for his car in a limping stumble.

"I declare, Manuel, if that's the way they're dressing in the big city now, I believe I'll stay a country bumpkin." Burke's loud comment echoed across the grounds.

Richard jerked open his car door. He stepped behind the door and stopped. "You'll regret this, Blaire Mackenzie." Richard tightened his tie, climbed in the car, and spun out down the driveway.

# fourteen

The whir of the newly installed fax machine woke Blaire the next morning. She climbed out of bed, stretched, then walked through to the office to see if a new order for ostriches had arrived. If so, she would have to let Burke know immediately. The fax machine had been her idea, and Burke loved the convenience. Prospective buyers could fax their orders rather than send them in the mail or via E-mail. This way Burke didn't even have to bother with the computer. Blaire quickly scanned the message:

> *Have found a prospective buyer for your ranch. Will be bringing the Wilsons to see the place this afternoon. Please try to be there to help show the place. I'm not familiar enough with your holdings to do a proper job. After this time I should be able to handle showings by myself.*
>
> *Janice Burns, Realtor*

A loud creak broke the silence as Blaire dropped into the office chair. A buyer? So soon? She hadn't expected that. What if they bought the ranch? She would have to leave. Would they want Isabel and Manuel to stay on? What would Burke do? Her heart ached. These people were her friends now. Startled, she realized she didn't want to lose them as friends. The loss would be too great.

"Wait a minute. What am I thinking?" Blaire got up and paced back into her room, the fax still clutched in her hand. "This could be the beginning of my dream. With the money

116

from this sale, I'll start my own office. I don't have to go back to Chicago. Any big city will do."

For several minutes she continued to talk with herself about the advantages of the sale. She felt as if she were trying to convince herself of something that wasn't right to do. She sank down on the bed and picked up her Bible. Smoothing her hand over the leather binding, she chewed her lip. *Lord, I don't want to go against Your will for my life. I'm not so sure about You wanting me to be anywhere else.* She turned to the familiar passage in Psalm 23. " 'He maketh me to lie down in green pastures.' " She ran a fingertip over the words as if that would help her understand better. "Lord, help me know for sure what You want. When these people are here today, make Your will clear. Thank You, Jesus."

She pulled on a pair of jeans and an old T-shirt. After freshening up, she headed for the kitchen. Manuel, just finished with his breakfast, stood and carried his dishes to the sink as she entered. Burke and Isabel sat across from each other. They all smiled at her. Blaire felt warmed. These people cared for her.

She tossed the crumpled fax on the table as she sat down. "I just got this fax. Janice Burns, the Realtor, is bringing a couple by to look at the place this afternoon." The warm atmosphere chilled. Burke's eyes darkened to a stormy aqua. His narrowed eyes and tightened jaw spoke volumes.

Blaire turned to Isabel. "I'll help you with chores and any cleaning that needs to be done, Isabel. They won't be here until afternoon."

Isabel patted her hand. A faltering smile began, then faded. "Thank you for the offer. I'll do my best to have the house ready for them."

Burke's chair scraped against the tile floor like chalk against a blackboard. He carried his dishes to the sink, then grabbed his hat from the hat rack and slammed it on his head.

Manuel shot an accusatory look at Blaire as he followed Burke out the door.

Blaire stared down at her hands, folded in her lap. A lump filled her throat. Tears burned her eyes. She felt as if she'd lost a good friend. *Why do I care so much what he thinks? I'm not interested in him. He works for me.*

"*Mija.*" Isabel's hand rested lightly on Blaire's shoulder. "I know you're confused about what you should do. I also can see how much you care for Burke. Trust Jesus, *Mija.* He'll show you what to do."

Hot tears trickled down her cheeks as Blaire lifted her head. She tried to say something, but the words wouldn't come. Isabel wrapped her arms around Blaire. For several moments, Blaire leaned against the comforting warmth of the older woman. Isabel handed her a tissue and stepped away. Blaire wiped her eyes and blew her nose.

"Thank you. I do want to do what's right. I'm not trying to hurt anyone."

Isabel sat down in the chair next to her and clasped Blaire's hand in her own. "I understand that. I think Burke is hurting. He feels something for you too."

"He does?"

"I've never seen him so interested in a woman. Maybe God brought you here to meet him." Isabel smiled, a far-off look in her eyes.

"That can't be, Isabel. I made the mistake of having a relationship with Richard when I worked for him. I won't make the same mistake again." Blaire stood and headed for the door. "I'll start in the hatchery. Let me know if there's anything special you want me to help with this morning." She closed the door firmly, forcing herself not to look at Isabel. She couldn't stand to see that she'd hurt her friend again.

❧

The afternoon sun was falling toward the western mountains

when Burke saw the white Cadillac easing down the driveway. Even at slow speed, the car created a cloud of dust in its wake. He could see Janice Burns's look of distaste as she pulled up in front of the house. A sprig of hope blossomed. Perhaps, if the Realtor disliked the place, the potential buyer would also be repulsed.

Janice stepped out and waved a hand at the settling dust. She adjusted her navy blazer, managing to look cool despite the heat. She walked around the front of the car, pausing to peer at the white paint as if to see how dirty her precious car had gotten on the drive out.

The passenger doors opened. A portly gentleman climbed out of the front, then turned to give his hand to the equally stout lady clambering out from the back. The pair reminded Burke of Tweedledee and Tweedledum from *Alice in Wonderland*. They wore identical white suits and matching royal blue shirts. Tall cowboy hats sat on white hair that curled out from beneath the brim. He blinked, wondering if he were seeing double. The main difference was the heavy turquoise necklace that clashed with the woman's shirt. Both had heavy turquoise bracelets and watches. Only the woman sported dangling turquoise-and-silver earrings.

Blaire stepped from the house. Burke couldn't take his eyes from her. The gauzy blue-flowered skirt and blouse she wore accented her trim form. He knew if he were close enough he would see the dazzling blue of her eyes made brighter by the outfit. She must have a curling iron, for her normally wavy hair curled lightly around her face. She didn't walk out to greet her company, she glided. He knew that she felt she was a klutz, but she had a grace few women ever attained.

"Good afternoon, Mrs. Burns. Did you have any trouble finding the house?" Blaire stretched out her hand to greet the Realtor.

Janice's smile looked a tad strained. "I don't think I realized quite how far away from town you are. I planned to get up here by myself, but the Wilsons were so enamored with your listing they insisted on coming out today." Janice made introductions, and Blaire shook hands with the rotund couple, Vern and Fran Wilson.

"This place is a mite off the beaten path to be asking so much." Vern Wilson waved a hand. The rings on his fingers sparkled in the sunlight. "I thought this was an ostrich ranch. I don't see many ostriches."

"Where is the main house?" Fran spoke like a bellows pumped her words out. "I'm surprised the employees' quarters are right here."

Blaire's back stiffened. "This is the main house." She gestured behind her. "This house is made of adobe and has been here for nearly one hundred years. My uncle redid the roof, replacing many of the rafters. If you would like to come in, I believe you'll be amazed by the western charm he achieved."

Fran leaned close to Vern as if to speak privately, but her words could have been heard in the next county. "I expected a mansion for the price. Where will our friends stay when they come to visit? I'll bet this house doesn't have the number of bedrooms we need when we entertain."

A red flush crept up Blaire's cheek. Her hands were clenched into fists. Burke leaned back against the trunk of the tamarisk tree where he'd been sitting in the shade doing some equipment repair. This couple didn't seem too sold on the place so far.

Vern stopped and leaned so far back Burke wondered if he would fall down. Of course, as round as he was, he might just bounce back up again. The comical thought made him bite his lip to keep from laughing.

"This tree has got to go." Vern pointed to the very tree Burke sat under. "First thing you know a tree like this will fall on the house. Someone could get killed." He shook his head and followed his wife through the door.

The urge to laugh had faded with the man's comment. Without this tree the house would be a furnace in the summer. Between the thick adobe walls and the shade of the huge tamarisk tree, Ike's home had always been a respite from the hot Arizona summers.

Leaning over his work, Burke tried to focus. For some reason all he could think about was Blaire. He'd been devastated this morning when she'd mentioned a buyer. For weeks, he'd pushed the possibility of her selling the place to the back of his mind. The longer he knew her, the more he wanted her to stay. Since the day they'd visited the zoo, he'd been struggling with his growing feelings for her. He knew women couldn't be trusted, but he'd also begun to pray. Now, he wanted to bridge the gap between himself and Jesus. He wasn't sure why that was important, but it was.

The door to the house opened. Blaire stalked out, then turned and waited. She held her right arm stiff against her side, fingers kneading the material of her skirt. Her curls were frizzed. He could almost picture her aggravated fingers combing through her hair. Noting the slight droop to her shoulders, the remnants of his anger faded. He wanted to hold her and let her know everything would be better soon.

Burke got up and sauntered toward the door. He knew without asking that Blaire would need his help for the next part of the tour. Her knowledge of the rest of the operation lay mainly in accounting. She hadn't had much experience at the plant.

"We could maybe keep this for a guest house." Vern thumped the wall as he walked out onto the porch. "It would take a lot of fixing up, but we could make this a real western treat. I think some of our guests would like the idea. Of course, it would take a total remodeling job. That means a lot of money."

"But, where would we live?" Fran breathed the words with a slow drawl.

"We'll just have to build ourselves a better house." Vern stepped away from the doorway, letting Fran out.

"What have we here?" Fran stared at Burke, standing a few feet behind Blaire. She lifted her hand and held it out to him like some medieval lady waiting to be kissed by a knight. Burke wasn't sure how she managed to lift her hand. Each finger held at least two huge rings. Her pinky couldn't possibly bend, being almost entirely encased in silver.

"This is my ranch manager, Burke Dunham." Blaire looked relieved to see him. She grasped his arm and pulled him forward.

"Ooh! Does he come with the ranch too?" Fran batted her mascara-laden lashes at him.

Vern tilted back his head and guffawed. "Just because the place is backward doesn't mean you can still own slaves, my dear."

Burke shook hands with Vern, then Fran. Afterward, he resisted the urge to wipe his hand on his jeans. With a gallantry he didn't know he possessed, he offered to show them the rest of the ranch and explain the way everything worked.

For the next hour, Vern grilled Burke about the details of raising, selling, and processing ostriches. Although the man looked empty-headed, his questions revealed that he had an astute business sense. Surprised by the depth of knowledge they disclosed, Burke wondered just how much homework the man had been able to do in the short time he'd known about the ranch.

When they reached the house again, Blaire invited the Wilsons in for something to drink. Isabel had some lemonade for them. Manuel was working on the evening chores. Burke started to excuse himself, but the look of pure panic on Blaire's face convinced him to stay a little longer.

"We must be heading back to Tucson." Janice stood and straightened her jacket. "Thank you for showing us around. This is quite an operation."

Vern lifted his bulk from the couch, then turned to help Fran to her feet. He pursed his lips and gazed up at the ceiling before looking at Blaire. "I like this place. I'm looking for a tax write-off. A ranch like this should do the trick. By tomorrow I'll have an offer ready for you. I'm sure I can make it worth your while to sell to me."

"You really want to raise those birds?" Fran paled a little as she stared aghast at her husband.

"No." Vern shook his head. "I'm sure we'd get rid of the ostriches. Cattle would be easier to manage. At least it would be easier to find help for a cattle ranch."

"But Uncle Ike worked hard to build this ranch. He specialized in the best ostriches."

Vern grunted and tugged at his pants. "Can't help that, my dear. We'd be a laughing stock with our friends if we had giant chickens around. Now cattle, those make sense to have."

Blaire's shoulders sagged as she walked her prospective buyers to the car. Burke slipped out the back door. He wondered if he needed to begin planning his future. He loved working with the ostriches, but it looked as if his time at this ranch was about finished. He wouldn't stay and work for the Wilsons no matter how much they paid.

# fifteen

The next evening Blaire wandered out to the porch. She hadn't slept well the night before. Burke had been gone most of the day. She wondered if he was avoiding her.

She trudged over to the porch and settled in the swing. Not having the strength to push, she sat still, contemplating the desert. A roadrunner darted down the hill, probably in search of his evening meal. She tried to picture him with a coyote chasing him down. Somehow, this small comical bird didn't match the long-legged fowl in the cartoon. The roadrunner paused, his head tilted to one side. He stretched out his neck and darted off into the brush.

The front door opened, and Burke stepped out. "Do you have dibs on the swing, or is there room for one more?"

She pulled her skirt closer and tucked it under her legs. "There's room."

The swing creaked as Burke lowered himself. He began to push, and Blaire found herself relaxing with the soothing motion.

"Isabel said supper will be ready soon."

"I think I'll pass. I'm not very hungry."

The quiet stretched between them. Blaire didn't have the energy to carry a conversation.

"What are you watching?" Burke lifted one arm and rested it on the back of the swing behind Blaire. She breathed deeply, trying to ignore the way her heart sped up at his nearness.

"There was a roadrunner over there on the hill. He ran in the brush, and I was wondering if he would come out."

Burke gazed at the brush for a moment. "He's probably

after some critter that's come out for its evening meal."

Blaire glanced at him in surprise. He turned to look at her, and she couldn't look away. For once he didn't have his hat on. Short, straw-colored hair looked as if he'd run his fingers through it recently. Aqua eyes perused her with a seriousness she couldn't take right now. His broad shoulder looked like a perfect place to rest her head and try to forget the troublesome decisions she needed to make. She forced her gaze away from his.

"In the cartoon the roadrunner always ate grain. You mean they eat meat?"

Burke tilted his head back and laughed. "In the cartoon the coyote always fell off tall cliffs and lived. I don't think it was meant to be very accurate. Do you know another name they have for the roadrunner?"

She glanced at him and shook her head. "I don't know anything about them."

He leaned closer. Her breath caught in her throat. His eyes twinkled as if he were aware of her discomfort. "They're called snake killers."

Blaire's mouth dropped open. "That was certainly never in the cartoon."

Burke grinned. "Actually, they eat rather large rodents for such a small bird. They eat mice and insects, but they also eat gophers and snakes."

"How do they kill them? They seem like rather timid birds."

"Are you sure you want to know?" Burke's eyebrows lifted. She nodded. "I once saw one snap up a gopher. The gopher struggled, but the roadrunner raced to a nearby rock and killed it. Then the roadrunner swallowed the gopher whole."

"That's disgusting." Blaire pushed against the porch floor, sending the swing a little higher. "I realize I'm from Chicago and know nothing, but there are some things you can't fool me on."

His eyes widened. He put his hand over his heart and gasped. "You're suggesting I'm not telling the truth."

She leaned toward him. "Yes."

The door opened and Manuel stuck his head out. "Supper's ready."

"Say, Manuel." Burke's call stopped him from closing the door. "How do roadrunners kill gophers?"

Manuel glanced at Blaire, then shrugged. "They beat them to death on rocks." He closed the door.

"He probably knew to say that." Blaire crossed her arms, refusing to be fooled.

Burke stood and offered her his hand. "You can ask Isabel or look it up on the Net."

Her hand fit perfectly in his. He closed his fingers over hers and tugged. She came off the swing more quickly than she intended. Her left leg, curled beneath her all this time, had fallen asleep. She stumbled. Burke wrapped an arm around her. She fell against him.

"Here you are, falling for me again."

She could hear the overtones of laughter in his voice. The scent of aftershave mingled with hay swirled around her. For just a moment, she allowed herself to lean against him. His arm tightened. She thought she felt his cheek brush her hair. Her leg began to tingle. She pushed away.

"I guess we'd better go in." She forced a smile. "You made me talk so much I've worked up an appetite." Blaire realized spending time with Burke had rejuvenated her. She didn't feel the weight she had earlier. She still dreaded the decisions ahead, but somehow she knew she was closer to understanding the right one to make.

The phone rang as they walked into the kitchen. Isabel answered, and Blaire could hear a woman's excited voice from the table across the room. Isabel handed the phone to her.

"This is your Realtor. She says the couple who were here

yesterday have made a good offer."

Blaire took the phone and turned her back on the table. She listened without comment, while Janice Burns gushed out the news of the generous offer. This was more money than she'd ever dreamed of having. Nothing would stand in the way of her dreams now. So why didn't she feel elated? Why was that sense of dread creeping back in?

"If you fax me all the information, I'll look it over and get back to you, Janice." She listened again. "Yes, I have your home phone. You wrote the number on the card you gave me. I may take the weekend to pray about this and call you on Monday morning." Janice wasn't happy with that decision. "I'm sorry. I'll let you know as soon as I can." Blaire hung up the phone. *God, You've got to help me with this. I'm so troubled. I want to live according to Your will, but the way just isn't clear. Help me.*

❧

Breakfast was on the table when Burke finally entered the kitchen the next morning. He wasn't usually this late, but he'd tossed and turned most of the night. Thoughts of what Blaire would do with the offer from the Wilsons kept him awake far into the night. He kept remembering how she'd leaned against him when he'd helped her up from the swing. The scent of her hair and the feel of his arms around her haunted him long after he should have been sound asleep. A part of him wanted to trust her. Another part screamed that he couldn't do that. She would sell the ranch, take the money, and they'd never see her again. He'd even prayed, but he wasn't sure God had heard.

"Good morning, Burke." Isabel dished up a plate of food for him. She squeezed his shoulder. Somehow he knew she understood his dilemma.

"Would you like to go to church with us this morning?" Blaire's bright smile surprised him. She must be excited about the sale. "You haven't gone in a long time. All those admirers you have keep asking for you."

Burke grinned. He knew the younger kids at church loved to play with him. "I guess they know a kid when they see one. I'll see if I can get ready in time." He cut a bite of the hash browns. He felt better. Maybe church would help him find the answer he needed. Perhaps this time would be different.

The service was about to begin as Burke followed Isabel and Blaire to their pew. Blaire stopped to hug some of the women and greeted others as they walked down the aisle. He couldn't believe how relaxed and friendly she was with the people after her stiff, formal entry the first time they'd come.

They sat down, and Burke glanced around, acknowledging several greetings from people he'd grown up knowing. He clasped his hands together, waiting for the old uneasiness to start. Instead, a sense of impending excitement coursed through him. Did the feeling have to do with something that was about to happen or was his awareness of Blaire the cause?

By the time Pastor Walker stepped up to the pulpit, Burke could barely sit still. He gripped his Bible to keep from wringing his hands. Every song they sang during the service spoke of one's trust in or walk with the Lord. He couldn't break away from the feeling that God had a special message just for him today. He shifted, bumping against Blaire for the umpteenth time. Blaire glanced up at him, and he shrugged. How could he explain this restlessness when he didn't understand it himself?

Pastor Walker turned once again to Psalm 23. Burke was surprised to find that after all the time he'd been away, they were still studying the same short passage of Scripture.

"This morning we're going to finish up the last of Psalm twenty-three. In fact, those of you who have been here for the whole study know we're going to look at the latter part of verse six: 'And I will dwell in the house of the Lord for ever.'

I'd like to start by clarifying some of the words in this passage." He pulled out a sheet of notes from beneath his Bible.

"Let's start with the word *dwell*. We all understand what it means to dwell in a house. I think most of us live in houses, so we assume the word *dwell* in this verse means to live in." He paused and looked at the congregation. "However, this word means more than to live in a house. This has a permanency as in the cleaving of marriage. It also carries a connotation of sitting in quiet, as in an ambush, or waiting. Then there's the word *house*. We all know what a house is. But this word *house* is to a building just like the word *church* is to a place. The church refers to a body of believers. Likewise, the word *house* in this verse is much more than a simple dwelling place.

"This passage is telling us to cleave to God. We can go to Him and sit quietly. We can trust Him with every aspect of our lives, not just with those parts we want to relinquish." The pastor leaned forward. His voice hushed. "God wants every part of you. He wants your hopes, your joys, your wants and needs, your expectations, and your fears."

Straightening, Pastor Walker stared down at his notes. "You know, this week I was reading again the story of Abraham and Sarah. Abraham is referred to as a man of faith, and he had a great faith. He followed God when no one else would. He left his homeland not knowing where he would go. He trusted God completely. . .for a time." Stepping out from behind the pulpit, Pastor Walker moved closer to the congregation. "What happened when famine came to the land? Abraham quit trusting God and went to Egypt."

The pastor stopped and rubbed the back of his neck. "This reminds me of our study of Psalm twenty-three, verse one. Remember the part that says, 'I shall not want'? God supplies all our needs according to His riches in glory as the Scripture says in Philippians chapter four, verse nineteen." He paused and gazed around at the congregation. "I looked this week and I couldn't find anywhere that says God will supply our wants. I wonder if Abraham had his needs met, but perhaps he had some wants that weren't being fulfilled." He grinned. "Maybe he wanted one of the new camels with the built-in TV/VCR." Everyone laughed.

"Whatever happened, Abraham decided to step out and take care of himself. He started trusting in himself rather than in God. When he got to Egypt, he lied about Sarah because he had misplaced his trust. He wasn't dwelling in God's house anymore."

The pastor's voice faded. Burke could feel the sweat beading under his shirt. Hadn't he accused God of not caring for his wants? Did he trust in God? From the time he was little he'd trusted in his mother, grandmother, and father. He'd thought he trusted God, but now he wondered. Was he expecting too much when he wanted to trust in Blaire? Was that an example of not trusting God?

Pastor Walker returned to the pulpit. "Let's look at the final words in this verse. . .'for ever.' " An expectant hush settled over the congregation. "Forever. All your life and into eternity. That's how long you're to dwell with God. That's how long you can trust Him with your life. He'll never leave you nor forsake you. He's always there. He wants what's right for you."

Closing his Bible, Pastor Walker carried it with him as he stepped down from the platform and stood in front of the people. "I want you to recall a time when you gave your whole life to God. I know you might be a Christian, but is there some part of your life you've withheld from God? Are you still trying to run things? Are you like Abraham, trying to head into Egypt rather than waiting on the Lord?"

Burke pulled himself up as the congregation stood and began to sing a hymn of invitation. He felt as if his fingers would make indentations in the pew in front of him. An urgency built inside him. He closed his eyes, trying to wait for the feeling to pass. Blaire began to sing, but he couldn't join her. As if from a distance, he released his grip on the pew and walked down the seemingly endless aisle to the pastor.

∂

Isabel's gasp startled Blaire. She glanced over. Isabel had tears in her eyes. Blaire followed her gaze and saw Burke talking to the pastor. She'd been so caught up in the song and message, she hadn't noticed him leaving. Pastor Walker took Burke's hand, and the two of them knelt in prayer. The people continued to sing.

Pastor Walker stood and held up his hand. The song ended. "Most of you know Burke. He's been coming to church here for a long time. As a youngster he asked Jesus to be his Savior. Today he's come to admit that although he's a Christian, he's never completely surrendered his life to God until today. I wonder how many of us are the same way? We trust in our salvation experience, but we still want to control the reins. We want to call the shots."

He smiled at Burke and squeezed his shoulder. "I'm happy to say that we have a brother here whose faith is strong enough that he can admit that mistake. He's ready to trust only in Jesus. I'd like to close in prayer, then ask you to come give Burke your blessing."

Moisture burned in Blaire's eyes as she closed them for the prayer. She knew what it meant to learn this lesson. She'd had to be humiliated by Richard to come to the point where she'd surrendered her life to God. After her decision last night, she had the peace of knowing He was truly in charge of her life too.

# sixteen

The aroma of enchiladas made Blaire's stomach growl as she walked through the door after church. "I'll be out to help you in a minute, Isabel." She headed into the bedroom to put away her purse and slip off her shoes. She wiggled her toes in the thick carpet and sighed. Home. She wanted this to be her home. She longed to stay here, but what if she missed the city? What would she do if the isolation grew old? Uncertainty crowded around. She needed someone to talk to.

When she walked into the kitchen, Manuel was busy setting the table, and Burke was filling glasses with ice water. Isabel insisted they drink a lot of water. She said that, in the dry desert, water was the most important ingredient of one's diet. Blaire had to agree with her. Manuel complained on a regular basis. He would love to have a soda with every meal, including breakfast.

"Let me help cut the lettuce or the tomatoes." Blaire stepped up beside Isabel at the counter.

Isabel glanced at the oven and relinquished the knife. "Okay. I'll set the enchiladas on the table." She wiped her hands on her apron. "I don't know what to do with all this help. I think you are all very hungry."

"We must be desperate if you're allowing Blaire to use a knife. Aren't you afraid she'll toss it across the kitchen?" Burke made a face at Blaire when she turned around to glare at him.

She shook the paring knife at him. "Now listen, Buster." Her words were cut short as the knife slipped from her wet fingers. She gasped as the point dropped toward her bare toes. The blade clattered to the floor a half-inch from her big toe.

132

Large hands grasped her upper arms and lifted her, moving her to one side of the cutting board.

"I think I'll take over here before you can only count to nine on your toes." Burke's eyes twinkled as Blaire smirked at him.

"You probably think that was an accident." She put her hands on her hips and tilted her nose in the air. "Well, I'll have you know, I might have been doing that on purpose. Perhaps I'm an expert knife thrower and was only trying to fool you."

He leaned close. His nose nearly touched hers. "Well, are you?"

She couldn't think. "What?"

"An expert knife thrower."

He straightened, and she caught her breath. She wanted him to come close again. She wanted to touch him, to have him hold her. Instead she reached for the knife. He pulled it away from her.

"Before I give you this deadly weapon, I want to know we're all safe."

Manuel chuckled. Blaire could feel her cheeks begin to heat. "If you'll kindly step back against the wall over there, I'll demonstrate my ability." She grinned as Burke glanced at the wall.

"I think I'd rather just sit down and eat. Perhaps you can tell us about your circus days when you threw knives at poor unsuspecting souls." He picked up the bowl of lettuce. "By the way, are any of them still alive?"

Manuel guffawed. Isabel chuckled. Blaire followed Burke to the table. "I know you won't believe me, but there's Jack." She sat down. "Of course, now they call him One-Eared Jack."

When the laughter died down, they said the blessing, then began to serve the food. Before anyone took a bite, the phone rang.

"I'm closest. I'll get it." Blaire crossed to the phone and lifted the receiver. "Hello?"

Her face lit up. "Clarissa? Where are you?"

Burke looked at Isabel. "That must be her sister." Isabel nodded.

"You're going to be where?" Blaire was practically jumping up and down. "I can't believe this. Of course I'll be there. Call me when you get in, and I'll come down for the day. Can you come to the ranch?" She was quiet a moment. When she spoke again Burke could hear the disappointment. "I understand. It'll be great to see you. We have a lot to catch up on. Okay. Bye."

Blaire slipped back into her chair and picked up her fork. Her eyes were bright, and her eyelids fluttered several times before she looked up. "That was my sister, Clarissa. She and her husband are back in the States on deputation." Her voice grew thick, and she cleared her throat. "They timed this to coincide with my wedding." She shrugged as if to say the reminder didn't mean anything to her. "They'll be in Phoenix at a church Wednesday night. Clarissa wants me to spend Tuesday with her. I hope you don't mind."

Isabel reached over and squeezed Blaire's hand. "Not at all, *Mija*. I'm sorry she won't be able to come out here, or at least that's what I gathered from your conversation."

"They have to be in northern California on Friday to speak at a missions conference. They'll have to leave early Thursday." She sighed and cut her enchiladas with her fork. "This is such a busy time for them. They need the support from the churches. I don't want to interfere with that."

Burke ate slowly, watching Blaire. He couldn't seem to take his eyes off her. A blond wave fell forward to partially cover her creamy cheek. Something had changed between them. Maybe the change was his, not hers. He shook his head and took another bite without tasting any of the spicy food. What was different?

He thought back to his commitment that morning. *Am I that changed, Lord? Is trusting You giving me the ability to also trust Blaire?* With complete clarity he realized this wasn't an issue of trusting Blaire. He only had to trust Jesus. *"Blessed is the man that trusteth in the Lord, and whose hope the Lord is."* Burke looked down at his plate as his grandmother's favorite verse from Jeremiah came back to him. She used to talk to him about putting his trust in God and not in people or land. Now he understood. As long as he trusted God with his life, he could trust a friend or wife without worrying. Yes, they might hurt him sometimes, but God would be there to help him through the rough times.

For the first time, he could recall Julie and what she'd done without feeling agonizing pain. Blaire wasn't anything like Julie. Oh, he'd seen the signs that Julie wouldn't stay true to him before he'd left for college, but he'd chosen to ignore them. When he came home expecting to prepare for a wedding, he hadn't known the wedding would be between Julie and his worst enemy from high school days. That hurt enough, but the cruel words and taunts from Julie cut so deep he'd thought he'd never heal. The laughter as she'd draped herself across Bill's lap and said, "You didn't really think I'd be serious about a ranch boy like you? I want a man who's going places."

Only now, through the grace of God, could he see the lies she'd told him for what they were. He'd confided his hurt over his mother's and grandmother's deaths to her. She'd turned that confidence into lies. "I don't know any woman who wants you, including your mom and grandma." Her words and actions had left him with a complete distrust of women. He'd decided then to never again allow a woman into his heart. How could he have been so blind? A lump wedged tight in his throat as he thought of the healing God had done during church that morning.

Manuel scraped the last of the food from his plate. "I'm taking off for awhile." He set his plate in the sink and headed out the door. Isabel sighed and shook her head. "You young people are always in a hurry to do things." She stood. "I'll clean up the kitchen, then go over to Ophelia's and check on her. I think she tries to do too much. Will you be okay?" She looked at Blaire, who nodded.

"I'll stay here and work on my cross-stitch or something equally exciting."

Burke cleared his throat. They both looked at him. His spoon slipped from his fingers and clattered to the floor. He felt like a nervous schoolboy.

"Been around me too long?" Blaire's eyes sparkled with laughter. Burke relaxed.

"Well, at least when I throw my spoon no one has to worry about losing an ear." He grinned and wished the table would disappear. Then she wouldn't be so far away. "I thought maybe you'd like to go down to the Gila River with me this afternoon. I know where some great blue herons are nesting." He held his breath.

Blaire smiled. "I've never seen a great blue heron or the Gila River up close. I'd love to go. Let me help Isabel with the dishes first."

"No, you two go on. I've got nothing better to do." Isabel flicked the dish towel at them. "It won't take long to get these cleaned up."

Burke pushed back from the table. "You might want to get on some different clothes. In some places the brush at the river is pretty thick."

"Aye, aye, Sir." Blaire gave a mock salute. "I'll meet you topside in twenty minutes."

He felt like a love-struck schoolboy as he watched her sashay out of the kitchen.

&

Blaire tightened her grip on the hairbrush. Her shaking fingers couldn't seem to keep their hold. She'd already dropped the brush twice in two minutes. "This is crazy. You're acting like a teenage girl going on her first date. This isn't a date. Burke just wants to show you some more of the wildlife around here. He's still trying to convince you how wonderful this place is."

She paused. In all the excitement of Clarissa calling, she'd forgotten her need to talk to someone about staying or leaving the ranch. Clarissa would be perfect. She gave her hair a final brush, checked her lipstick, and headed for the door.

Burke was waiting in the swing, moving it in a gentle rhythm. He stood when she came out of the house. The swing jerked away, then came back and stopped against the back of his knees. He didn't seem to notice. He stared at her. Blaire glanced down, expecting to see something disgusting staining her shirt or jeans.

"I haven't eaten since I changed, so I know I didn't spill anything on me. Did I smear lipstick somewhere?"

Burke started. A red flush crept up his cheeks. "I'm sorry. The blue shirt—and your eyes. . ." He moved his hat back on his head. "You look nice." His green gaze caught and held hers. "Ready to go?"

Blaire followed him to the pickup. Already misgivings were starting to knot her stomach. What was she doing? Was she going with Burke to see these birds and the river or did she just want to spend time with him? Maybe she should back out now. Burke swung the truck door open and turned to offer her his hand. All thoughts of staying home fled. She placed her hand in his and climbed in the cab. A tingle of excitement flowed through her even after Burke released her hand and closed the door.

"How will we get down to the river? Every time I've been

past on the highway, the drop seemed pretty steep. Are there roads?"

Shifting gears, Burke headed down the drive. "There are a few roads that lead down to public places on the river, but I don't usually go there. The river passes through my dad's ranch. I have a private place where I like to go."

Blaire tried not to stare at Burke as he drove. Although she managed to keep from turning her head, she still watched his strong hands on the steering wheel. She knew the work he accomplished with those hands, yet despite the strength in them, she'd seen how gentle he could be with the baby ostriches and the kittens. Burke was so complex. *I could spend a lifetime getting to know him.* The thought startled her. She forced her eyes and thoughts away from the man beside her.

The road down to the river turned out to be a dirt track. Gnarled limbs of mesquite trees swept out far enough from the trunks to provide shade. Burke stopped the truck under a tree not far from the river.

"Here we are." He shut off the engine and smiled at her. Tension crackled in the air.

Blaire opened the door and stepped out. She could hear the soothing ripple of the river nearby. The shade and the water cooled the temperature. She took a deep breath. The air held a fresh scent of wet sand and earth.

"This is so pretty, Burke. I'll bet you bring a lot of people to this place."

His smile was almost shy. "Actually, you're the first."

She stared. "Why is that?"

He shrugged, then took her hand and led her closer to the river. "When I was a boy, this was a special place I came to when I wanted to be alone."

She wanted to ask a million questions, but somehow she knew the time wasn't right. His short statement gave her plenty to think about. "Do you go swimming here? Is the river deep enough?"

They stopped close to the edge. Water rushed past, swirling around rocks and tree limbs.

"I don't like to swim in the Gila." Burke stepped close. "I've known too many people who drowned in this river. They didn't realize the danger with the tree limbs and brush below the surface along the edge. Either that or they fought the current rather than traveled with it."

Blaire was silent, staring into the suddenly deadly looking water. "I didn't think about desert rivers being so dangerous."

"Most places in Arizona have dry river beds rather than rivers like the Gila. Every year in the rainy season, people get caught in flash floods in the riverbeds. In fact, the Tucson rescue teams come up to Winkelman to train for flood rescues by using the Gila."

Burke squeezed her hand. "I didn't mean to talk about something so depressing. Come on." He lowered his voice to a whisper. "If we're quiet, we can see the herons." He led her downstream along a narrow trail that wound beside the river. After about fifty yards he halted. Stepping to the edge of the bank, he pulled her forward.

"Do you see them?"

Blaire looked across the river. All she saw were weeds and water. The river flowed fast, cutting under the bank on the far side. Standing on the edge of the bank, leaning out, gave her the feeling of standing on the rushing water. Blaire shook her head to indicate she couldn't see the herons. She didn't want to scare the birds by talking.

Stepping closer, Burke put his arm around her and pulled her back against his chest. He put his cheek next to hers and with his hand on the other side of her face directed her gaze. Her heart pounded. She fought the feelings welling up inside. She wanted to ignore the birds and pretend she couldn't find them just so Burke would keep his hold on her. A flutter of movement on the opposite side of the river caught her attention. The weeds swayed. A tall, blue-gray bird with a long slender beak and stick-like legs stood watching them. Blaire sucked in a breath. The bird tilted its head to one side as if deciding what they were doing. With a regal air, the bird stalked gracefully downstream through the flowing river.

She turned to look at Burke. He straightened. His arm stayed around her, pulling her close. She couldn't look away. The bird faded into the background. Burke leaned closer. Blaire closed her eyes. She felt his arms tighten around her. Her hands rested lightly against his shirt. She leaned forward.

His lips touched hers. The ground moved beneath her feet. She'd never felt a kiss like this. She felt like Alice falling down the rabbit hole. Burke gasped and tightened his hold. Their bodies splashed into the river.

## seventeen

As the cold water wrapped around them, Blaire realized the earth really had moved under her feet! The Gila River's strong current pulled Burke and Blaire apart. She would have panicked, but Burke wrapped his strong fingers around her arm and wouldn't let go. He tugged on her, towing her to the surface.

"Put your feet down. You can stand up."

Blaire fought the current and discovered the water only came to her thighs. Like a young child demanding attention, the river dragged at her legs. Burke stared past her, a look of longing on his face. She turned and saw his hat bobbing in a wild dance on the surface of the water.

"Your hat." She tried to look remorseful. She couldn't do it. One glance at the freshly crumpled bank that had tossed them into the river brought home the hilarity of the situation. Blaire slapped a hand across her mouth, trying to hold back the laughter. She peeked at Burke. He watched her with a silly grin.

"That was some kiss, wasn't it?"

Blaire couldn't hold back the laughter. She leaned against Burke and laughed until tears mixed with the river water on her cheeks. She could feel the vibration of Burke's unrestrained mirth.

Burke pushed her away. She looked up at him. His hair, still mostly plastered to his head, was just starting to spring upright in comical little toothpicks pointing skyward. She lifted a hand to her head. She must look just as bad.

"Shall we stay here all day or are you done swimming?"

She looked down river, pretending to be in deep thought. "Since I forgot my raft, I believe I'll quit for the day."

Burke waded to the bank, placed his hands on the grass, and started to hoist himself out of the water. Another piece of the edge gave way. He tumbled into the water with the dirt and came up sputtering. Wiping away the water, he grinned at her. "I guess I wasn't clean enough. That'll teach me not to forget my weekly bath."

He headed for the bank again, this time examining the place he'd chosen to climb out before he placed his weight on it. Once on firm ground, he turned and reached a hand down to Blaire. His fingers were nearly as cold as hers, but their strength felt good. With one quick tug, she left the river behind and stood next to Burke, water streaming from her clothes into the grass. The warm sun felt good on her face.

Burke slipped an arm behind her back. His other hand cupped her cheek. His eyes, darkened with emotion, held hers in a powerful gaze. "I think there's something we didn't finish." His voice turned husky. He tightened his grip.

Everything in her ached for his embrace. Blaire tilted her head back. She leaned forward. A picture of Richard flashed through her mind. She closed her eyes. She could see the E-mail he'd sent, telling her the engagement was off. Pain ripped through her heart.

Burke's warm lips covered hers. She jerked her head back. Stiffening her arms, she pushed away from him. Ignoring the hurt in his eyes, she backed off. Burke let go of her.

"I think I need to go back home and change into dry clothes." She knew the excuse was lame. She wanted to fall back into his arms, but she couldn't do that. She refused to go back on her promise to herself. Never again would she fall for someone she worked with.

Burke stared at Blaire as she paused to squeeze water out of her blouse. *What did I do wrong? One minute she seemed to be enjoying my company, then this.* He ran a hand through his damp hair. A foreign feeling welled up inside. Remembering his vow at church that morning, he stared down at the ground. *Lord, I know I promised to give You complete control of my life. I meant that, but now I've taken matters into my own hands again. I'm sorry, Lord. I know I've fallen in love with Blaire. I'm not certain how she feels. Help me know what You want me to do. Thank You, Lord.*

He cast a longing gaze down the river where his hat had disappeared, sighed, and headed for the truck. His wet jeans weighed a ton. At least he had a spare hat at home.

❧

"Who would have thought Phoenix traffic would be so bad?" Blaire slammed on the brakes as a red sedan darted in front of her. Gripping the wheel, she glanced in the rearview mirror and flipped on her turn signal. She needed to switch lanes to get on 101. A string of bumper-to-bumper vehicles refused to part. "Come on. I need to be in that lane." She tried to move over. The blare of a horn made her jerk back into her lane. She passed the exit for 101.

"I can't believe this." Blaire felt like pounding the steering wheel. She hadn't seen the sign for the exit because of her concentration on all the heavy traffic. Now she would have to get off and work her way back. She was following Burke's directions to get to northwest Phoenix, where her sister was staying. If there was an alternate route, she didn't know what it was.

A knot formed in her stomach. Keeping her turn signal on as traffic slowed to a near standstill, she tried to move over lane by lane. Getting off the freeway turned out to be tedious work. She was three miles past the turnoff for 101 and completely worn out before she reached an exit ramp.

By the time she pulled into the parking lot of the motel where Clarissa and her husband, Jim, were staying, Blaire felt weak from exhaustion and nerves. She climbed out and headed into the office to check in. Clarissa had arranged for them to have adjoining rooms.

"Blaire, it's so good to see you." Clarissa enveloped her in a hug. When she pulled back, Blaire could see the sheen of tears in her sister's eyes.

"It's been too long, Clarissa. Sometimes I wish Jim were pastoring a church in the States where we could see each other now and then. I miss you so much."

"Not half as much as I miss you." Clarissa pulled her inside the room and shut the door. "Jim has adjusted to missionary life better than I have. I still struggle with the language and customs. I always seem to say or do the wrong thing." She gestured at a table and two overstuffed chairs on wheels in the corner of the room. "Come on in and sit down. Do you want a soda or something?"

Blaire sank into a chair and tried to relax. "You can't imagine how awful the trip here was. I don't ever remember fighting traffic like that."

"What?" Clarissa pulled out the other chair and sat down. "Don't tell me the queen of the freeways managed to be intimidated by a few cars."

Blaire grimaced. "To think I used to live in Chicago where this traffic would be a joke. I didn't think anything of the delays. Now I feel like I've been run over by a truck, and I wouldn't have the energy to drive back home if the house was burning down." Her head dropped back against the chair, and she closed her eyes.

Cinnamon curls bounced as Clarissa shook her head. "Does this mean our shopping trip is out? I'm dying to get to the mall with you."

One eye cracked open. "Did you say mall?"

"Yep. The magic word." Clarissa smirked.

"Where's Jim?"

"He's spending the day with the pastor. They're doing

door-to-door evangelism in the neighborhood around the church, hoping to get more people to come for the service." Clarissa leaned forward, a wicked grin crossing her face. "He won't be back before suppertime. We have all day for the mall."

Blaire raised her hands in surrender. "All right, I give. Bring on the shopping." She pushed up from the chair. "My car or yours?"

"Definitely yours." Clarissa grabbed her purse and the room key. "Jim has ours, and I don't want to walk."

Finding a parking place that was within walking distance of the stores proved to be a challenge. After cruising several aisles, Blaire spotted a car backing out. She wheeled into the space before anyone else could beat her to it.

Inside the mall, chaos ruled. "I haven't seen this many people in months." Blaire had to lean close to Clarissa to talk. The rumble of people conversing could have rivaled the sound of an approaching freight train.

"Where do you want to start?" Clarissa looped her arm through Blaire's. She pointed toward a trendy shop. "Oh, look, fake jewelry." She grinned. "And it's the cheap kind I can afford. Let's go."

For the next two hours they visited jewelry stores, bookstores, and clothing shops. At noon they edged through the crowds, looking for the food court. They stood in the middle of the open area in front of the various restaurants, perusing the variety of foods offered.

"What are you going to have?"

Clarissa brushed a stray curl from her forehead. "Something totally American. It has to be disgusting too." She giggled. "I still crave cheeseburgers. I haven't gotten enough of them."

Blaire laughed. "Cheeseburgers it is then."

"With bacon."

"Whew, that is disgusting." Blaire raised her eyebrows in mock dismay. "Does it get worse than this?"

"Yes." Clarissa's eyes sparkled. "I want French fries and onion rings."

Blaire grabbed the back of a chair near them. "I think my heart is clogging." She wrapped her arm through Clarissa's and tugged. "I see the eatery of your dreams right down here."

A few minutes later they had worked their way back to the tables with a fully loaded tray. "I can't believe I let you talk me into milkshakes on top of all this other fat. I won't be able to eat anything but celery for a week." Blaire squeezed past a group of teenagers dressed in a style only they could appreciate. She set the tray down on an empty table.

The teens milled around, communicating more with shrugs and gestures than words before wandering off. Blaire glanced at Clarissa, whose troubled gaze followed the kids.

"I think every teen and preteen in Phoenix is here at the mall today." Blaire motioned to the milling throng passing through the food court.

"It's sad, Blaire. These kids get in so much trouble because they have no direction in life. Sometimes I think Jim and I are in the wrong country as missionaries. I wonder if we shouldn't come back here and try to minister to the youth in the cities. They sure need someone."

Blaire swallowed a sip of her milkshake. "You know, I used to think shopping at the mall was the only place to be."

"You don't anymore? When did this change?"

"I didn't realize I'd changed until I came down here to see you." Blaire stirred a fry in the ketchup. "I guess I used to think only of me. Shopping fulfilled something I needed. Today, there's no excitement like there used to be."

"I'm boring you? Is that what you're saying?" Clarissa's astonished expression was almost comical.

"No, I'm glad to be with you. I just don't enjoy the crowds

and noise like I used to. The same thing happened on the freeway this morning."

"So, what is it you want?" Clarissa turned serious and leaned back in her chair.

"You know I wish you had time to come out to the ranch."

"Are you changing subjects on me?" Clarissa's eyebrows raised. "Why would I want to see this ranch? I thought you were going to sell out and move back to the city."

"I thought so too." Blaire pushed her half-eaten sandwich away. "Something's changed. I'm thinking of keeping the ranch and living there."

Clarissa's mouth dropped open. "You, the all-time city girl, are going to live in the middle of nowhere with a bunch of birds? What brought this on?"

Blaire watched the milling crowds of teens and preteens as they wove in an intricate pattern along the mall walkway. She wanted to talk to Clarissa. They'd always had an easy rapport, but somehow she didn't know how to put her feelings into words. As always, Clarissa waited patiently.

"I know for years you've allowed God to lead you wherever He wanted you to go. Even when you married Jim and went to the mission field, you've always seemed to know exactly what God wanted you to do."

Clarissa's eyes widened. "Do you really believe that? You're talking like God wrote specific instructions for us and we've followed them to the letter."

"Well, you always seemed so confident. Have you ever doubted?" Blaire hesitated, stirring her straw in her milkshake. "Have you ever argued with God?"

A light, tinkling laugh drifted across the table. Clarissa's eyes sparkled with mirth. "You have no idea how I've argued with God. Which time would you like to hear about? The time we got to the village and found we were to live in a little hut with a dirt floor? Or when evening came and the hordes of bugs began eating us alive? What about the time I picked up a pot to cook in and found it occupied by a snake?" She shook her head. "I sometimes think all God hears from me are complaints. I keep telling Him how unsuited I am for the mission field, but then He shows me how I've made a difference in the lives of the women I've worked with. Maybe I haven't seen hundreds of people led to salvation, but I've taught cleanliness. There's less disease now than when we first came. The children don't have as many sores. Eating habits have improved. And they can all quote Scripture, and they want to hear Jim preach."

Blaire laughed. "Okay, okay, I think I get the picture."

"Now, tell me what you've been arguing about with God." Clarissa leaned forward, resting her elbows on the table.

A group of blue- and purple-haired teens strutted past. A young mother marched by towing a screaming toddler. Blaire sighed. She used to love the anonymity of the mall crowd. Today, the clamor and confusion irritated.

"Do you think we could continue this conversation back at the motel room? I'm getting a headache from all this racket."

Pushing back her chair, Clarissa began to clear the trash from the table. "I think that's a great idea. Maybe we should stop by an emergency medical center and have you checked out. I've never seen you leave a mall without buying something."

Blaire tossed her half-eaten sandwich in the trash bin and slid the tray on top. "Boy, you're tough on me today. Since you're insisting on junking out, I'll go buy us a couple of giant cookies to munch on this afternoon." She indicated the shop at the end of the row that sold cookies decorated with any message you wanted. "I'll get a regular size one and get you one of the platter-sized ones."

Clarissa grinned and patted her slender hips. "Sounds good to me. I'll take chocolate chip and a peanut butter too. Cookies have been in short supply lately."

"I heard a report that in Tucson some sort of group was experimenting with using worms in cooking. I guess they have lots of protein and are plentiful. They even had worm cookies. Maybe we could get the recipe, and you could teach Cookie 101 in your village. Sounds very healthy. Just think of the nutritional value." Blaire couldn't help laughing at her sister's horrified expression. "Come on, Clarissa." She looped her arm through her sister's and headed to the cookie shop. "I was only making a suggestion."

# eighteen

The door to the motel room barely clicked shut before Clarissa tore open the sack of cookies. Their sweet, spicy scent filled the air. She pulled out a huge peanut butter cookie, broke off a piece, and popped it into her mouth. "Oh, this is heavenly." She paused in her chewing and glared at Blaire. "I think there is a conspiracy here. By the time we head back to the mission field, I'll have to have all new clothes."

She broke off another piece, then pushed the bag closer to Blaire. "Have one, Sis. Save me."

"I don't think you have to worry." Blaire pulled out a chocolate chip cookie. "Mom said you'd lost weight, and I agree. You can put on several pounds and still look great."

Clarissa groaned. "This is a conspiracy. You should have seen the food Mom foisted off on me while we stayed with them. It's a good thing we're only on deputation for a few months." She brushed a cookie crumb from her blouse. "Now, tell me about your argument with God. The last I heard you were waiting for Him to show you what He wanted you to do. You talked about starting an accounting firm. What happened to that idea?"

Blaire spread out a napkin and began breaking her cookie apart in small pieces. "When I first heard about my inheritance, I thought the ranch was my answer to prayer. Then when I arrived, I found it was different from what I had pictured. I didn't want to keep the ranch. I wanted to sell out and move back to the city. I could take the profits and start my accounting firm."

"So what happened?"

"There were people involved. Uncle Ike had people working for him, and I couldn't disappoint them and just thrust them out in the cold, so to speak. I promised to stay for awhile, learn the workings of the ranch, then sell."

"You've been here almost six months. Isn't that long enough to learn about the ranch?"

Popping a piece of cookie in her mouth, Blaire chewed slowly. "I don't know what happened. It's kind of a long story."

Clarissa shrugged. "We've got time."

Blaire began telling her sister about her arrival in Arizona and her introduction to the ostriches and the residents of the ranch. "I felt so bad for Isabel and Manuel that I couldn't sell the ranch right away. Then there was the pastor's message."

"Umm. The story builds. What message is this?"

"He spoke on Psalm twenty-three, verse two and how God places us in green pastures, but we don't always see them that way. I keep thinking about that Scripture and wondering if this isn't the green pasture God has for me. If I leave, will I be giving up a blessing, or is this just the means to attain my blessing? I get so confused."

Clarissa leaned forward and placed her hand on Blaire's knee. "God isn't the author of confusion. I think He's making His will plain for you, but outside influences and perhaps you yourself are creating the confusion."

Blaire nodded as Clarissa sat back in her chair. Blaire set a chocolate chip on her tongue and sucked until it melted.

"What else?"

Why did her sister have to know her so well? Blaire struggled with her feelings a minute, then spoke in a soft voice. "There's Burke."

Clarissa's eyes lit up. She leaned forward again. "Burke? The ranch manager?"

Blaire nodded. Silence stretched between them.

"Do I have to sit on you and tickle you like you used to do to me so I'd tell you everything?"

Blaire laughed and made a face at her sister. "No. I'll talk even without your threats. I'm just not sure how to begin or what to say."

"Do you have feelings for Burke?"

Blaire nodded.

"Like you had for Richard?"

"No." Blaire was surprised at her emphatic answer. Clarissa leaned back in her chair and looked pleased.

"Good. We all knew Richard wasn't right for you, but there was no way to convince you of that. Now tell me about Burke. And don't you leave anything out. If you do, I'll know."

She was right. Clarissa had always known if Blaire was keeping secrets.

"The first time I met Burke there was a spark between us. I tried to ignore him. I even tried to dislike him." She sighed and wrapped her fingers together. "Nothing worked. He's wonderful. He works hard, he's fun and funny, he's sensitive and sweet."

"Whoa, is this a man or a saint?"

Blaire smirked. "Let me think for awhile, and I'll tell you a fault." She tapped her finger against her chin. "Oh, yes. I know. He hates computers."

"What? You're interested in someone who doesn't like computers. Perish the thought." Clarissa placed her hand over her heart and collapsed back in her chair. Then she grinned and sat back up. "Okay, so he's Mr. Perfect. How is his walk with God?"

"He's been a Christian since he was a young boy, but just last Sunday he went forward at the end of the service and admitted he had never surrendered his life to Jesus. He's had a rough life, but in the last two days I've seen a change in his attitude. He's happier, more content, I guess."

"You're making this hard." Clarissa shook her head. "Mom's going to want a full report, and I won' t be able to give it. I wish I had time to go to the ranch and meet this perfect specimen."

"There's a problem, though." Blaire stirred the cookie crumbs on her napkin.

Clarissa held up a hand. "Don't tell me. He's not interested in you, right?"

"No. I think he's interested. In fact, I'm sure he is."

"So what's the problem?"

Blaire hesitated. "I made a promise to myself that I would never date someone I worked with again. After Richard, I realized that only creates problems. This is a point of honor, I guess."

"You could fire him." Clarissa grinned. "I can see it now." She placed a hand dramatically on her brow. "Burke, Honey, you're fired. Will you marry me?"

Blaire wadded up the empty cookie bag and threw it at Clarissa. "Cut it out. You would die if I asked some guy to marry me rather than waiting for him to ask. I remember your lectures on being a proper lady. What happened to that?"

"I guess I've been on the mission field so long, I've changed. You know, over there the women hit the men on the head and drag them off to get married."

Blaire's eyes widened. "Do they really?"

Clarissa crossed her arms over her stomach and doubled over with laughter. "Of course not. You're as gullible as you were when we were kids."

"Give me that bag back so I can throw it again." Blaire held out her hand. Clarissa grabbed the bag up and stuffed the missile behind her back.

"Seriously, Blaire. Do you think Burke is anything like Richard?"

"No, but I'm still scared of the commitment."

"Can you be content living without your accounting business?"

Blaire raked her fingers through her hair. "That's a funny thing about the ranch. This is such a big business that the books call for an accountant's skill. I've also thought about offering my services to other ranches in the area. For instance, Burke's dad has a big ranch, and maybe he could use an accountant. I would enjoy doing that."

Clarissa steepled her fingers under her chin and watched Blaire.

"You know, I almost feel like Uncle Ike knew me better than I know myself. It's like he planned all this, and all I had to do was take the time to realize how right Arizona and the ranch are for me."

"I don't know about Uncle Ike, but I know God knows you best. He's the one who's had all this planned out." Clarissa reached across the table and caught Blaire's hands in hers. "Blaire, trust Jesus with everything. Don't be afraid of making the same mistake you made with Richard. You're a different person, and from the sound of things, so is Burke. If God brought you together, perhaps you should listen to Him."

Blaire stared at her sister's fine-boned hands. Was Clarissa right? Was this another area where she was trying to maintain control rather than following God's path? *God, help me to follow You completely. I don't want to mess things up again. If Burke is the one You've chosen for me, please let me know. Let him know too, God.* A surge of excitement and anticipation ran through her. Waiting one more day to get home felt like an eternity.

৵

Burke went to hang up the phone and missed. Shaking his head, he focused on where the headset should be placed and hung up.

"Who was that?" Isabel peeked in from the front room where she'd been dusting.

Burke tried to wipe what he knew must look like a silly grin from his face. "It was nothing." He rubbed his jaw, forcing the giddy feeling down. "Say, Isabel, I need to do some business. I'll be back after lunch sometime."

She frowned at him as if she suspected something was going on. "I'll let Manuel know."

"That's okay. I'll talk to him before I leave. I have some instructions for him."

"Burke, that real estate lady called again, asking for Blaire. She said the Wilsons are determined to buy the ranch, but Blaire says she doesn't want to sell now. They've made a better offer. Does this mean Blaire intends to stay?"

Burke frowned. "I don't know, Isabel. I hope she doesn't want to sell, but we can't make her stay. This has to be her choice."

Isabel smiled. "I'm glad you've gotten a peace about that, Burke. I believe Blaire wants to do what's right. She's not like Julie."

"I know." Burke sighed. "I guess for years I blamed God for everything bad that happened to me. I thought He was punishing me for something I did wrong or because He didn't like me. I know that's not true now, but when you're hurting, you can believe a lot of things." He ran his finger around the brim of his hat. "Then when Julie hurt me and blamed me for what happened to Mom and Grandma, it was too much. I can see I needed Jesus as the Lord of my life instead of putting my faith in people. I'm glad I've got peace about it now too."

"What a lesson to learn." Isabel patted his shoulder. "In marriage, you need to trust Jesus first, then trust your wife."

Burke chuckled. "Good point, but who said anything about marriage?" Settling his hat on his head, Burke strode to the door. "See ya later." Blaire would be home later today, and based on that phone call, he had plenty to do before she got back.

❧

Blaire left late Wednesday morning for the trip back home. After making several shopping stops and grabbing a quick bite of lunch, she headed out of town. As the freeway turned once more into a divided highway, then finally a two-lane road, she breathed a sigh of relief. Tension drained from her back and shoulders. Her hands relaxed on the wheel. A wave of longing washed through her. She couldn't get home fast enough.

"Lord, what have You done to me? I'm even missing those crazy birds." Blaire thought of the stories she'd told Clarissa and Jim last night, keeping them all laughing for hours. They especially loved the story of Sprinkles flying over the fence. Jim, who didn't like cats much, said the ostriches must have good taste. She chuckled again thinking about it.

A picture of Burke popped into her mind. Of course, he hadn't been far from her thoughts since she'd come to Phoenix. She couldn't believe how much she'd missed him. Every time something happened, she found herself wanting to share the experience with him. "Lord, I love him so much. I thought I would never love anyone again. You were right to bring me here. I feel like I've found the other half of who I am. I know I hurt him last Sunday when we were at the river. Please, help me to make amends."

Warmth suffused her as she recalled Burke's kiss. She had never been kissed like that, or maybe she'd never felt that way about a kiss. "You know, Lord, what I'd like most is a husband who will pray with me about things. I've seen Dad and Mom pray together for years. I know Clarissa and Jim do too. If a marriage is going to stay strong these days, the couple needs to be able to come before You together." She wondered about Burke. At first, he'd seemed so uncomfortable with the things of God. In the last two days, he'd changed. Would he be willing to pray with her? Would he put God first in a marriage? Somehow she knew he would.

The miles skimmed by. Blaire loved the mountains and cactus-covered hills as she drove between Superior and Kearny. Tired of sitting in the car, she almost stopped in Kearny for a soda, but the thought of home drew her like a magnet. She didn't stop until she pulled into the driveway and parked near the house.

*I've been gone a day and a half, and I feel like it's been weeks. I must be going crazy.* Blaire's heart pounded. She couldn't wait to talk to Burke. She needed to tell them all about her decision to keep the ranch and go on living here. She wanted to apologize; she wanted to take up on the idea in Clarissa's joke and drag Burke off by the hair. She giggled. He'd be furious if she bent his hat, even if the one he wore now wasn't his favorite.

"I'm home." Blaire listened to the echo in the house. No one answered. She carried her overnight bag in and plunked it on the bed. Planning to unpack later, she walked through the kitchen, wondering where everyone was.

A thud greeted her as she stepped out the kitchen door. She heard voices coming from the small house Burke and Manuel shared. Stepping around the tamarisk trees, she saw Burke in the back of his pickup accepting a box that Manuel was handing him. She crossed the yard toward them.

"What's up?"

Manuel and Burke both jumped. Manuel greeted her, then trotted inside and shut the door. She thought she heard Isabel's voice from inside the house. Burke put his hand on the side of the truck and vaulted over the side.

"Hey, how was the trip to Phoenix? Did you have a good visit with your sister?"

She eyed the boxes and furniture in the bed of the truck. "I had a great time. What are you doing?"

"I'm moving out."

"What?"

"I'm going to stay with my dad for awhile." Burke reached for her, and she stepped back. All the well-planned speeches flew away.

"Blaire, I've talked to Manuel. He knows the procedures of the ranch nearly as well as I do. He's going to take over for me if that's okay with you."

"Why would he need to take over for you?" Blaire felt like her mind wasn't working right. Dread crept up and wrapped around her heart.

"He needs to take over because I'm quitting." Burke didn't look at all remorseful over his announcement.

# nineteen

Burke winced inside at the pained expression in Blaire's eyes. He wanted to kick himself. How could he have been so blunt? He'd planned his speech. The words were outlined in his head. He even knew the place where he would take her to explain why he was quitting and how he felt about her. Would she listen to him now? He didn't think so.

The glint of tears shone in Blaire's eyes. She whirled and stalked toward the house.

"Blaire, wait." Burke's mind raced. She halted but didn't turn around. "My dad is having a barbecue for some family and friends this weekend. He wanted me to make sure everyone here would come. Isabel and Manuel already know. Will you come?"

She half turned. Her blond hair lifted in the breeze. "I don't know." Her voice sounded hoarse, almost strangled. Blaire continued to the house, stepped inside, and shut the door with what sounded like measured care. Burke strode toward the house. He had to talk to Blaire and explain. He had to tell her the real reason he quit.

"Hey, Burke, we'd better get going. This is the last load. I have to get back in time to do the evening chores." Manuel came out of the house lugging a heavy box. "Mom said your dad called and wants you there right away to help him with something too."

Pausing midway between the two houses, Burke felt a tug of war on his heart. He needed to keep his word to his dad and Manuel, but he needed to explain to Blaire too.

"Ready?" Manuel called. The box he carried plunked onto

the bed of the truck.

Swiveling back to the small house, Burke stuck his head in and called to Isabel. She answered from the room he'd used as a bedroom. He waved to Manuel to let him know he'd be right there, then stepped inside the house.

"Isabel." Burke pulled the hat off his head and ran his hands along its brim. "I didn't think Blaire would be home so soon."

"She's here already?" Isabel sounded as surprised as he'd felt.

He nodded. "She wanted to know what I was doing, and I told her I quit. She didn't give me a chance to explain why. I know I hurt her. Can you please talk to her? Try to get her to come to Dad's barbecue, please. I'll call and come by, but I'm not sure she wants to see me right now."

Isabel put down the rag she'd been using to dust the room. "I'll talk to her, *Mijo*. You go see what your dad needs. Come back tomorrow and talk to Blaire. Okay?" She patted his hand and accompanied him to the door.

Settling the hat back on his head, Burke glanced at the silent house where Blaire had disappeared. He turned back to Isabel. "I'll call tonight if I can. If not, I'll be by tomorrow." He slammed the truck door behind him. The motor roared to life. Even the ostriches made him feel guilty. They stared at him as if he'd done something wrong.

❧

Blaire sank to the floor by her bed. She pulled her knees up and rested her head on them. Tears that she'd been holding back from Burke's view began to soak her skirt. *Why, God? Why did this happen again?* The bed shook with the force of her sobs. *You brought me here to a supposedly green pasture. Is this it? If this is a green pasture of Your making, why am I hurting so much? Why did he leave?*

The pastor's voice seemed to echo through her mind. "The

Lord makes us lie down in green pastures." Well, maybe this wasn't where God wanted her to be. Perhaps she'd been mistaken. Had God been mistaken?

A knock echoed through the room. Isabel called through the door. "Blaire, are you okay?"

Reaching for a tissue, Blaire blew her nose. "I'm fine, Isabel. I'm a little tired from the trip. I'll be out later."

Isabel was silent for a long minute. "We'll talk when you've rested. Don't miss supper."

Crawling up on the bed, Blaire stretched out. She pulled her worn, stuffed giraffe next to her and curled around it. Was there something wrong with her? At least Burke hadn't run off with a Vanessa. Or had he? As the speculations raced through her mind, exhaustion took over, and she drifted off to sleep.

The spicy scent of chili wafting under her nose woke Blaire. She stretched, slightly disoriented. Was Isabel fixing chili for breakfast? That would be strange. Loosening her hold on her giraffe, she opened her eyes and sat up. Her skirt, full of wrinkles, wrapped tightly around her legs. The late afternoon sun poked weary rays through her window. The earlier hurt came rushing back.

Climbing off the bed, Blaire determined to shower and get ready for supper. She'd prayed that God would show her why He'd allowed this to happen. She wanted to blame God, but deep down she knew He didn't want her to be hurt again. Perhaps Burke had a reason for quitting and running off like he did, but she wasn't ready to hear his excuse. She planned to stay far away from the handsome ranch manager who'd stolen her heart.

&

For the rest of the week, Blaire managed to avoid Burke. When he called, she told Isabel to tell him she was busy. She was usually working on the books or at some other job so she wasn't lying, but she could have stopped and talked to him. She didn't want to. Just when she'd come to terms with her feelings for Burke and had been ready to let him know she loved him, he'd done an about-face. Had he only pretended to care about her?

Early Saturday, Isabel began making mounds of potato salad and salsa to take to the barbecue at the Dunham ranch. Blaire helped cut vegetables, working quietly beside the chattering Isabel. She didn't want to go to the party, but she couldn't think of a reason to stay away that wouldn't offend Burke's dad. Scraping the peelings and vegetable waste together, Blaire headed for the door to dump them on the compost heap.

"You're awfully quiet, *Mija*."

Blaire jumped, scattering onion and potato peels across the kitchen. She set the pan on the floor and began to grab the stray parings. Keeping her back to Isabel, she hoped the subject would be dropped.

Isabel stooped and began to help clean the floor. "Are you okay?"

Blaire swiped at her eyes with the back of her wrist. "I'm fine. Sorry I spilled this on your clean floor."

"I'm not worried about my floor." Isabel picked up the refilled pan and set it on the table. "I'm worried about you. You haven't been the same since you came back from Phoenix. Is it because of Burke quitting?"

The lump in her throat kept Blaire from talking. She shrugged. Picking up the pan, she walked to the door. "I'll be right back." Her voice came out a hoarse whisper. She slipped out the door before Isabel could say anything.

The phone rang as Blaire returned to the kitchen. Afraid Burke was calling her again, she motioned to Isabel that she didn't want to talk and went to her room. Sinking down onto her bed, she picked up her Bible and ran her hand over the familiar cover. *Lord, thank You for the green pasture You've put me in. It hurts right now, but I've come to understand that You have a purpose in having me here. Help me to trust You completely with my heart, my life, everything.* She wiped a tear from her cheek.

Putting the Bible back on the nightstand, she stood and crossed the room to look at the pictures on the mantel. One was a picture of Uncle Ike holding her on his lap, taken years ago. She smiled. A feeling of contentment washed over her.

"Uncle Ike, you were right. This is the right place for me. These wide-open spaces have brought healing to my soul. I love the people here, the quiet." She laughed. "I even love those crazy ostriches. Thank you."

⁓

The pickup truck bounced hard as Burke accelerated down the dirt track leading back to his dad's house. This was the most important day of his life, and he was late. All he'd had to do today was check the mineral licks set out for the cattle at various stations. That had gone well until early afternoon when he found the cow down with a broken leg. Not wanting to waste the meat, he'd field dressed her and climbed back in the truck. Then he'd hit a section of road that had been washed out in one of the summer rains. He'd taken more of his precious time rebuilding the road so he could pass the washout and continue on. Finally, when he thought he might not be too late, the truck had had a blowout. The spare had refused to come free. He was filthy, tired, and certain his dad's barbecue would be over before he arrived.

His fears were laid to rest when he eased down the steep hill across from the ranch house and jolted across the dry creek bed. More than twenty cars still packed the parking area near the house. Burke pulled around to the side away from the festivities. He backed up to the cooler where his dad always hung meat to cure. This time of year the cooler was off, but the big motor would get going quickly. He had to hang the cow's carcass before he could clean up.

The aroma of barbecued meat, rolls, and home-baked pies filled the air as Burke stepped from the house a bit later. He ran a hand through his damp hair and wished he'd worn his hat. Somehow he felt naked without it. His stomach growled, reminding him of how long he'd gone without food. Breakfast was a distant memory.

"Burke, where have you been?" Isabel waved at him from where she sat with her friend Ophelia.

He smiled and waved, his eyes continuing to scan the crowd. He couldn't see Blaire anywhere. Moving over to where Isabel and Ophelia were chatting, he greeted them, chafing at this need for small talk.

"Mmm. The food smells delicious. I'll bet you made half of it Isabel. Is there any of that famous barbecue sauce of yours?"

"You know that's not really my barbecue sauce. It's your grandmother's recipe. Irene's Barbecue Sauce. Your father gave me the recipe years ago to make for these barbecues."

"And you make the best." Burke gave her a kiss on the cheek."

"Well, I had help today. Blaire helped with all the cooking."

"Isabel, where is Blaire?"

The two women glanced around at the crowd. "She was here talking with us not long ago." Isabel's brow furrowed. "You know she said something about wanting to walk. She also mentioned kittens."

"Thanks." Burke strode away toward his dad's barn.

"Wait, Burke, don't you want something to eat? Your dad said you've been gone all day with nothing to eat."

"I'll be back for some food." Burke couldn't stop the grin on his face. He felt like a kid headed for the cookie jar.

The musty scent of grain and hay greeted Burke as he stepped into the dim interior of the barn. Burke paused to let his eyes adjust. Soft laughter drifted out from behind a pile of loose hay. A sense of anticipation settled over him. At last, he would have the chance he needed to talk with Blaire.

"Oh, poor baby. I can still feel the little kink in the end of your tail. Do you have nightmares of giant birds tossing you up in the air?"

Burke crept closer and watched as Blaire lifted the half-grown calico cat and rubbed her cheek against Sprinkles's fur. From the way she pressed her ear close, he knew she could hear the motorboat purr as Sprinkles expressed appreciation for the attention.

"I sure hope these cows treat you better than the ostriches did," Blaire murmured as she stood, still holding the cat in her arms. "I'd better get back and see if Isabel is ready to go. I need to get back home."

Sprinkles climbed up and wrapped herself around Blaire's neck. Her tail draped under Blaire's nose like a giant mustache. Blaire reached up to rub the cat's head.

Burke chuckled. "What's your hurry?"

Blaire screeched. Sprinkles arched her back and hissed. Blaire whirled around. The cat jumped down and dashed off into the shadows. "I need to go." Blaire stepped to one side.

Burke moved to block her way. "We need to talk."

She folded her arms. "I think you made yourself quite clear when you quit without notice. Now if you'll excuse me. . ." She edged closer to the door.

Burke stepped to the side, bringing them almost nose to nose. "Blaire, I'm sorry. I know I hurt you, but I'd like a chance to explain. I've been trying to talk to you all week."

"I don't think we have anything to say to each other." She stepped away. She looked like a caged tigress ready to pounce.

"Please stay. I have so much I want to say."

The anger was beginning to fade from her eyes. "Such as. . ."

Trying not to breathe a sigh of relief, Burke took a deep breath. "Such as all I've been doing the last few days is praying about our relationship. Such as telling you how much I love you."

Her eyes widened. Her mouth dropped open.

"You know, I was only following the suggestion your sister made when I quit."

"My sister? You don't even know my sister. What does she have to do with this?"

"Clarissa called me after you left Phoenix. She said you would never consider marrying anyone you worked with. She told me how you want to do accounting for the ranchers around here. We had a long talk. I'm sorry I hurt you. It wasn't my intention. I was so surprised when you showed up early that I handled it poorly."

Blaire's eyes widened. She looked outside. Burke thought he saw a glimmer of understanding dawning in her eyes. "I didn't give you a chance to explain. I was so afraid you were leaving me that I rushed into the house. I should have listened to you."

Burke gave her his best repentant-little-boy look. "Will you forgive me?"

Sprinkles wound her way around Blaire's leg. Blaire tapped her finger against her lip. "Hmm. I'll forgive you on one condition." At Burke's questioning look she continued. "You have to forgive me too. And," she added, tilting her head to one side, "I'd really like you to repeat what you said a minute ago."

"You mean the part about your sister?" Burke tried to remember what he'd said.

Blaire took a step closer. "No, I mean when you were saying the 'such as' part."

"Hmm. That wouldn't be the part where I said I love you, would it?"

She nodded.

He lifted his hand and cupped her cheek, marveling at the softness of her skin. He wanted to grin but was too nervous. "We have something else to talk about. I know we've both been hurt and may have trouble trusting each other. I'd like to pray together often. I know if we build a relationship on Jesus Christ, He will help us through any rough times we might have."

Fumbling a small box from his pocket, Burke dropped to one knee. Blaire looked down at him. Tears glistened in her eyes.

"Blaire, will you marry me?" He popped open the small ring box. Lifting her hand, he kissed the tips of her fingers. "I love you. I've prayed about this so much. Will you be my wife?" He held his breath and waited.

She nodded.

He slipped the ring on her finger. The stone sparkled even in the dimness of the barn.

"Yes." The rasp of her voice startled him. "Yes." She sounded stronger. She tugged on his hand, and he started to stand. "Yes, yes, yes." She leaped forward and threw her arms around his neck. The unexpected weight threw him off balance. He tumbled backward. Blaire fell with him.

The force of the impact knocked the breath from him.

"Burke, are you okay?" Blaire grasped his face in her hands. His arms came up to encircle her.

"I must say I do like your enthusiasm, my dear." He grinned and pulled her close for a kiss.

"Meow." Sprinkles poked her head between them. She climbed on Burke and lay down across his neck, purring like a runaway motorboat.

"Does this mean I need her permission too?"

Blaire giggled. "You bet."

# epilogue

A trilling cacophony from the birds outside the window woke Blaire. Cool morning air wafted across her cheeks. She pulled the covers closer and snuggled in their warmth. Her eyes refused to open, but she sensed the source of the warmth close beside her and moved that way. She snuggled against the body next to her. The tangy scent of pine trees mingled with the spice of cologne.

Throwing her arm across the bare chest, Blaire nestled closer. Arms closed around her, holding her tight. She cracked one eye open and gazed up at Burke. His green eyes looked dark in the morning light. He lifted her chin and kissed her.

"Mmm. Nice." Blaire reached up to stroke his cheek.

"Good morning to you, Mrs. Dunham."

Blaire closed her eyes. "It's not morning yet. I'm still sleeping."

"Do you always talk in your sleep?"

"Mm-hmm. Ask Clarissa sometime. We used to share a room."

"Well, I think I should wake you up." Burke ran his fingers along her sensitive ribs.

She twisted and gasped. "Stop that. This is my honeymoon, and I'm sleeping in."

He chuckled. The tickling fingers attacked again. "This is my honeymoon too, and I want to get up and do some of the hiking we planned."

"Burke, stop that." Blaire twisted away, giggling. She forced her eyes to stay closed. "You're not supposed to wake someone who's talking in their sleep."

"I've never heard that." Burke's laugh sounded sinister.

"This is like a sleepwalker. You aren't supposed to wake them, either. It could damage the psyche or something."

"Hmm. This is getting interesting. I've never seen a damaged psyche."

The bed dipped. Blaire opened her eyes to catch Burke in mid-leap. She squealed and tried to roll to the side. She was too slow. Burke caught her and began to tickle. Blaire did her best to move away, but her legs got tangled in the covers. Before she knew what happened, she was wrapped up in a cocoon. Still Burke tickled. She laughed so hard tears rolled down her cheeks.

"Stop that. I'm awake."

"Are you crying uncle?"

"Never."

Before Burke could start finding her ticklish spots again, she twisted to the side. Instantly, she realized her mistake. Only empty air stood between her and the floor. Blaire hit the ground with a thud that would have hurt except for the pad of blankets and sheets wrapped around her. She looked up. A pair of sea-green eyes, round as saucers, stared down at her. She began to laugh all over again.

"Are you okay?" Burke poked the rest of his head over the edge of the bed.

"You looked so funny." Blaire gasped for air. "You reminded me of a little boy caught doing something he shouldn't."

Burke grinned. "Well, I don't think a husband is supposed to make his wife fall out of bed on their honeymoon." His eyes twinkled with mischief. "Now that you're awake, can we go hiking? These mountains are beautiful. We might even see some deer."

"I can't. I'm feeling all wrapped up."

Burke scratched his chin and looked thoughtful. "You

know, if I pick up one corner of that blanket and give it a hard yank. . ."

"Don't you dare." Blaire tried hard to glare at him. "All right, help me out here, and we'll go hiking. But if you continue to tickle me, I'll feed you to the ostriches when we get home."

Burke slid off the bed until he was on the floor beside her. He kissed her softly. "An ostrich a day won't keep me away."

Blaire freed an arm and reached up to cup his cheek. "That's the best news I've heard all day."

# *A Letter To Our Readers*

Dear Reader:

In order that we might better contribute to your reading enjoyment, we would appreciate your taking a few minutes to respond to the following questions. We welcome your comments and read each form and letter we receive. When completed, please return to the following:

Rebecca Germany, Fiction Editor
Heartsong Presents
PO Box 719
Uhrichsville, Ohio 44683

1. Did you enjoy reading *An Ostrich a Day* by Nancy J. Farrier?
   - ☐ Very much! I would like to see more books by this author!
   - ☐ Moderately. I would have enjoyed it more if

   _____

   _____

2. Are you a member of **Heartsong Presents**? Yes ☐ No ☐
   If no, where did you purchase this book?_____

   _____

3. How would you rate, on a scale from 1 (poor) to 5 (superior), the cover design?_____

4. On a scale from 1 (poor) to 10 (superior), please rate the following elements.

   _____ Heroine       _____ Plot

   _____ Hero          _____ Inspirational theme

   _____ Setting       _____ Secondary characters

5. These characters were special because_____

_____

_____

6. How has this book inspired your life?_____

_____

_____

7. What settings would you like to see covered in future
   **Heartsong Presents** books?_____

_____

_____

8. What are some inspirational themes you would like to see
   treated in future books?_____

_____

_____

9. Would you be interested in reading other **Heartsong
   Presents** titles?          Yes ❏          No ❏

10. Please check your age range:
    ❏ Under 18          ❏ 18-24          ❏ 25-34
    ❏ 35-45             ❏ 46-55          ❏ Over 55

Name _____

Occupation _____

Address _____

City _____ State _____ Zip _____

Email _____

# CALIFORNIA

*I*n the largest, most diverse state in the Union, four women—unique in their God-given talents and goals—share a common desire to find love.

Watch as God's Spirit leads each woman to discover where true love and fulfillment are to be found. Rest in knowing that "all things work together for good to them that love God—to them who are the called according to his purpose."

paperback, 464 pages, 5 ³⁄₁₆" x 8"